MEAN STREETS

My thanks are due to Joe, Nancy and Laramie Moore,
of the Moore Ranch in Bucklin, Kansas, for their good company,
great advice and astonishing ability to take this greenhorn
and make him vaguely saddleworthy

First published in the UK in 2010 by Usborne Publishing Ltd., Usborne House,
83-85 Saffron Hill, London EC1N 8RT, England. www.usborne.com

Copyright © Graham Marks, 2010

The right of Graham Marks to be identified as the author of this work has been
asserted by him in accordance with the Copyright, Designs and Patents Act, 1988.

Cover illustration by Sam Hadley.

Extract on page 221 from *The Charge of the Light Brigade* (1854) by Alfred Lord
Tennyson.

The name Usborne and the devices ♀ ⊕ are Trade Marks of Usborne
Publishing Ltd.

A CIP catalogue record for this book is available from the British Library.

JFMAMJJA OND/10   02166/1 ISBN 9781409522522

Printed in Reading, Berkshire, UK.

MEAN STREETS
THE CHICAGO CAPER

GRAHAM MARKS

USBORNE

1 7.15 A.M., AUGUST 15TH 1928, TOPEKA, KS

T. Drummond MacIntyre III, son of T. Drummond MacIntyre II (Senior Vice President of MacIntyre, MacIntyre & Moscowitz Engineering, of Chicago, Atlanta and New York City), sat on his horse, Biscuit, and watched the dogs bring the last of the cows across the dirt road from one field into another.

Trey (as he was generally known by one and all) got down, draped the reins over the fence and set about closing both gates. He could almost *smell* the bacon he knew Gramma Cecilia would be cooking, along with eggs over easy and hash browns, and his stomach growled and rumbled in anticipation. He'd been up since before 6.30 so he was somewhat ravenous.

Job done, Trey got back on Biscuit, whistled for the dogs and set off back towards the ranch house, just a short ride away. He'd been down at the Circle M – Gramps's spread just outside Topeka, Kansas – for almost a month now and there was no doubt that life on the ranch was about as far from the day-to-day to and fro of Chicago as it was possible to get.

And none the worse for that, he reckoned as he rounded a bend in the road and saw a very unusual sight – for the time of day and this neck of the woods as his gramps would say; some hundred yards or so up ahead a *very* classy white automobile had stopped. It looked like it'd been jacked up, and someone, who'd taken their jacket off and rolled up their sleeves, was kneeling down by one of the rear wheels. The other side of the dirt road, three men in sharp pin-striped suits and slicked-back hair were smoking cigarettes and seemingly in deep discussion.

As he got nearer, Trey could see that the man kneeling down was doing something to the wheel, and getting pretty mussed up in the process. Easiest thing in the world to get a flat tyre on these roads, he thought to himself as he got nearer.

"Mister!" Trey called out. "You need a hand?"

The men smoking glanced up, then went back to whatever it was they were talking about, but Mr. Shirtsleeves stood, wiping his hands on a grubby cloth, and shook his head. "No thanks, bud," he called back. "Almost done here."

Trey could see the dogs were getting interested in what was going on up ahead and he whistled them back to him as the tallest of the three suits ground his cigarette out with the toe of his highly polished black-and-white shoe, and crossed over to the car with one of his colleagues – a pale man who was wearing a pair of heavy-framed tortoiseshell spectacles.

As he approached, Trey saw that what he had here was a very fancy Buick Monarch, its black Landau top and streamlined coachwork covered in a layer of grey Kansas dust; definitely not the type of vehicle you saw very often in these parts. Being, it would not be exaggerating to say, *very* keen on automobiles, Trey knew this particular model had a six-cylinder 4.5-litre engine that developed 2,800 rpm; not quite as big as his Pop's 4.7-litre Chrysler Imperial, but no slouch. And he could see that the owner had opted for the wooden 12-spoke wheels, and the whitewall tyres that, if he remembered correctly, came with aluminium hubs.

He was about to stop for a look and a friendly chat,

the way everyone did in these parts, when he noticed the Buick had Illinois plates...but his attention was snatched away by the sight of the third suit, a shorter guy, walking across the road and flicking his lit cigarette behind him.

"Hey!" Trey yelled, without thinking, pulling Biscuit up.

"You mean *me*?" The man stopped and looked up at Trey, frowning. "Who you think you are, punk? Talking to me like that..."

The man's aggressive tone of voice and heavy scowl wasn't missed by the dogs, particularly Blaze, who started growling, his hackles right up.

"One of them mutts touches me, kid," the man started to reach into his jacket, "I'll make it sorry, so help me..."

Trey froze, his eyes wide and seemingly glued to the man's hand, knowing it must be a gun he was going for. All he could think of was how he would tell Gramma Cecilia if anything happened to one of her dogs. Then he somehow managed to break the spell of fear. "Blaze!"

"Stub the butt out, Frank. This ain't Chicago."

Trey glanced to his left and saw the taller of the two suits by the car coming towards him. He could tell that Biscuit had picked up on the rising tension, and was aware of the dogs nervously pacing near him. Feeling that his control over the animals was in danger of slipping away from him, all he wanted to do was get on his way before he lost it completely.

"You hear me, Frank?" said Tall Suit. "You could start a fire out here, right, kid?"

Trey looked at the man who'd just spoken, aware that his face seemed oddly familiar. "Yeah," he nodded, trying to figure out why he recognized him, "you bet."

The short guy didn't move.

"What I tell you, Frank?" Tall Suit raised his eyebrows questioningly. "Stub it out, *capiche*?"

"Sure. Anything you say..." Frank's lip curled, revealing a snaggle of yellowed teeth, and he shot Trey a filthy look as he crossed back over the road.

"I apologize for my associate, he doesn't spend too much time in locales such as these that don't have pavements. And thanks for the offer of help. Much appreciated." Tall Suit grinned, his smile wide and apparently friendly. He began to walk away, then stopped and turned back. "One thing, how far are we from this place – the T-Bone ranch?"

"Not so far, mister." Trey nodded down the road. "A couple of miles is all, you can't miss the signs they have up."

"Good to know." The man gave Trey a mock salute. "Thanks."

9

Trey glanced the other side of the dirt road and saw the one called Frank stamping around in the dry grass. Frank looked up and caught Trey watching him. His eyes narrowed as he stared back at Trey and spat like he really meant it into the dust.

"I see you again..." he whispered as he passed by, close enough for Trey to smell his oddly flowery cologne; his face was split by a humourless smile as he drew a finger slowly across his throat, leaving the sentence unfinished.

Gathering his reins up, Trey kicked Biscuit into a gallop and made tracks, his heart beating like a jackrabbit's back leg, his mouth drier than a sand pie...

2 A CALL IS MADE

Trey made it back to the Circle M in double-quick time. He could hardly believe he'd just been threatened with death by some mobster! As he rode he kept on seeing the man's gesture, his finger drawn like a knife blade across his throat; truthfully, he had thought people only did that kind of thing in the movies.

None of what had just happened seemed possible, and as the ranch house came into view Trey was still trying to make sense of things. Coming across the type of big-wheel gangsters who got their faces plastered all over the front pages of the *Herald-Examiner* newspaper back in Chicago (heck, they even got their pictures in the *Tribune*, the altogether far more serious paper his pop disappeared behind every morning at the breakfast table) was not what you expected out here in the country.

So, exactly what was a car full of hoodlums doing driving down the back roads of Shawnee County, Kansas? Because, if you believed everything you read in the popular papers (or what his father, rather scathingly, in Trey's opinion, called the yellow press), these types were more likely to be found in the big cities, making and selling illegal booze and blasting away at each other with tommy guns, than out here in cattle country.

For as long as Trey could remember there had been this thing called Prohibition, which meant it was against the law to drink – not stuff like Pepsi-Cola and root beer, but real beer, gin and bourbon whiskey and such. He'd grown up with his gramps – a dyed-in-the-wool Democrat (his own description) – telling anyone who'd listen, and plenty who didn't want to, that he thought it was a hare-brained Republican party idea to stop a man having a glass of his favourite tipple.

Quite a few times Trey had seen his grandfather wag a finger at someone daring to express an opposing view, telling them in no uncertain terms that Prohibition hadn't stopped *anyone* drinking, it had just let gangsters make a fortune selling illegal booze on the black market. It was one of the few subjects that Gramps and Gramma Cecilia, who never drank anything stronger than the occasional home-made sarsaparilla, disagreed on.

Riding under the wide-arched gateway, with the big Circle M brand up on top, Trey thought it curious that the men hadn't stuck to Route 66 instead of taking the back roads. They could, of course, have come to fill someone with lead, or put a guy in a pair of concrete boots, or merely scare the living daylights out of them. The man called Frank certainly looked like the type who did that kind of thing on a regular basis. But who would they do that to round here? And why?

Biscuit knew the way blindfolded round to the rear of the ranch house where there'd be some feed, so Trey let the pony take over while he continued to puzzle over what gangsters were doing so off the beaten track. It wasn't as if this place was buzzing, what with the nearest neighbours being at least a couple of miles away.

It was a mystery, and there was nothing that Trey liked more than the idea of being involved in a mystery. He believed – the same as his favourite private detective, *Black Ace* magazine's Trent "Pistol" Gripp –

that "the need for answers was in his blood". Although questions that desperately needed answering had very definitely been missing from this stay with Gramps and Gramma Cecilia. Mind you, he thought, as he tied Biscuit up to a rail, it meant he'd had plenty of time to pore over the book he'd saved up and sent for by mail order. He'd seen *How to Become a Private Eye in 10 Easy Lessons*, by Austin J. Randall, advertised at the back of *Black Ace* magazine, and, as the quote on the book's dustjacket said, it definitely was "A veritable mine of useful information".

Somehow the sight (not to mention the smell) of plates piled high with strips of crispy bacon, eggs, hash browns and, this morning, fried mushrooms and tomatoes, pushed all thoughts of Chicago gangsters from Trey's mind. For the moment.

By the end of breakfast, while he was helping Gramma Cecilia clear the table, it all came back to him as he picked up Gramps's empty plate.

"Guess what, Gramps," he said, watching his grandfather fill in a crossword clue in the *Topeka Daily Capital*'s puzzle.

"I try not to guess, son. I prefer to know..." He looked at Trey over his half-glasses and raised one eyebrow.

"Six letters: S-blank-blank-M-blank-E; another word meaning 'thwart'. Any ideas?"

Trey shook his head.

"Too bad...now what were you saying?"

"Want to know who I saw out on the North Road this morning with a flat tyre and looking for the T-Bone ranch?"

"Stymie!" T. Drummond MacIntyre, the first – known to close friends as Ace – sat back in his chair, smiling.

"What?" Trey frowned.

"It's the answer to a clue, dear." Gramma Cecilia took the plate away from Trey. "For heaven's sake, Theodore, put that silly game down and listen to what Trey is saying to you."

"It is *not* a silly game, Cessy, it's vital brain exercise!" Gramps tucked his pencil behind one ear and turned to Trey, nodding. "Vital, mark my words, son. Now who was it you saw with a flat tyre?"

"Well, I'm pretty sure it was a bunch of hoodlums, Gramps."

"Come again?"

"You know, mobsters? Like Al Capone?"

"You saw Al Capone out on the North Road, son?" Gramps looked over his glasses, a twinkle in his eye.

"No, Gramps, not *him*!" Trey knew he was having his leg pulled and was anxious to be taken seriously;

after all, it had seemed pretty serious back out there. "They had a brand-new white Buick Monarch, with Illinois plates, wood-spoke wheels and all!"

"I'm sure there are *no* people like *that* around *here*, dear..." Gramma Cecilia cleared the place mats off the table and disappeared back into the kitchen. "Thankfully, Chicago is five hundred miles away."

"It's five hundred and *seventy*, Cessy," Gramps called after her.

"Don't split hairs, Theodore..."

"But Gramps, I've seen people just like 'em in the papers, I'm *sure* of it!" Trey didn't think it a wise move to explain about the Death Threat, grown-ups having a tendency to overreact somewhat in such situations. "There were three of them, and a driver, and one of them was a real goon called Frank, and—"

"Well, you may well be right, son." Gramps got up, pushing his chair back, and pulled a gold pocket watch out of his tweed waistcoat to check the time. "And woe betide them if they come *here* looking for a glass of water – your gramma will give them a piece of her mind they won't forget in a hurry! Now come on, son – we both have places to go, people to see and things to do, have we not?"

* * *

16

Ace MacIntyre waited until his grandson had left the ranch house and his wife was busy with something in the kitchen before he went into his study, closing the door behind him.

Sitting at his roll-top desk he pulled open a drawer and took out a small, linen-bound notebook, flicking through its pages until he found what he wanted. Putting the notebook down, he picked up the telephone handset and tapped the bar, taking the pencil from behind his ear and doodling while he waited for someone at the local exchange to come on line.

"Is that you, Mr. MacIntyre?"

"Sure is."

"And what can I do for you today?"

"Put through a person-to-person call, please?"

"That'd be a pleasure – what's the number?"

Referring to the notebook, Gramps read out the number he wanted and then sat back listening to all the clicks, buzzes and hums it took to complete the connection. Finally he heard the sound of the phone ringing at the other end and he put the pencil down. Robertson Ely Bonner – Bob to his pals, "Behind Bars" to those he caught – was one of his oldest friends, and now headed up the Chicago branch of the Bureau of Investigation. Since Prohibition had begun, some eight years ago, Bob had become a *very* busy man, the "no drink" legislation, in both their opinions, having done nothing but give mobsters carte blanche to ride roughshod over the law.

"Yes?" The voice at the other end was crackly but clear.

"Bob? Ace MacIntyre."

"Son of a gun! To what do I owe this pleasure – you back in town and looking for a game of golf?"

"No, still out in the boondocks looking after cattle. Be back for Christmas, probably, to spend some time with the family."

"And how is everyone?"

"Fine, fine…" Gramps took a cheroot from the cedarwood box on the desk, struck a match and puffed it alight. "Fact it's because of my grandson, Trey, that I'm calling."

A chuckle came down the line from Chicago. "Oh yeah? What's he gone and gotten himself up to?"

"He *says* he saw some mobsters on the North Road this morning, early, while he was out doing chores. Seemed pretty sure, too, said there were three of them, and a driver. Considering Trey says he spotted an Illinois registration on the car, I thought you might like to know."

"Yes siree and yes indeedy…got no idea who they were, have you?"

Gramps tapped some ash off the glowing tip of the cheroot. "Not a one, but I *can* tell you where they were asking directions for."

"Saving the best till last, I see. Well?"

Gramps coaxed the cheroot a bit with a couple of puffs, blowing aromatic smoke out of the corner of his mouth. "The T-Bone ranch, Bob."

"You don't say…"

"I surely do."

"What I wouldn't give to be a fly on the wall down there right now, so's I could find out who these guys are."

"I'll keep my eyes and ears open, Bob. Best I can do."

"Be much obliged if you would, Ace, much obliged. You know trouble's been brewing since this last April, and it ain't going to cool down any till after the election."

"Never a truer word…" Gramps sat back in his chair, thinking of the shenanigans that had occurred during the Republican primaries in Chicago in April. Things had come to a pretty pass when political disagreements were settled by throwing hand grenades! Two leading politicians, and the racketeer Diamond Joe Esposito himself, had been killed. "You think we've got ourselves some trouble down here, Bob?"

"You mix up politicians with mobsters, there's *always* going to be trouble, Ace. Always…" Gramps heard a sigh come down the line. "You *sure* your boy saw what he says he saw?"

"I'd bet on it."

"He's a pistol, that Trey – no doubt be running the whole Bureau one day, he goes on like this."

"I'm sure he wouldn't mind that."

"You hear anything else, you be sure to let me know, okay? I'll be speaking to you, Ace, and be sure to give my best to Cecilia."

"Will do, Bob."

"And make sure to tell Trey to keep well clear of the T-Bone. Don't want him poking his nose around when those types are involved, no siree."

"You think I should send him home?"

Bob paused before replying. "No...no, I'm sure everything'll be fine. Keep in touch."

"Count on it."

Gramps put the handset down, relit his cheroot and sat back in his swivel chair, frowning as he thought about the last few moments of conversation. He wanted to ring Bob Bonner straight back and ask him what that pause had really meant, but he knew that his friend had only told him what he was allowed to. There was, without a doubt, something odd going on down here and he couldn't get rid of the feeling that trouble was more than just in the air; it was here...

3 ROUND UP!

All through the rest of the day Trey had wondered about his gramps's reaction to the news that he'd seen gen-u-ine, front-page-news mobsters. Disinterested hardly described it. He had not said anything else about the matter again and now, sitting up in bed, torch in hand and listening to the night sounds – owls and suchlike – Trey was doing what Austin J. Randall advised all aspiring detectives to do in *Chapter 2 – Basic Skills*. He was "Reviewing All The Facts", such as they were, which was not an awful lot. Trey looked at what he'd written in his notepad:

1 – Tall Suit (seemed an okay guy, considering),
plus:
- *Shirtsleeves (friendly)*
- *a sidekick named Frank (unpleasant)*
- *and one other man (pleasant), pale, with glasses.*

All four seen on the North Road this a.m. – early!

2 – Their Buick had Illinois plates, which <u>must</u>
mean they'd come from Chicago (mustn't it?).
Where else would they have come from?

3 – <u>If</u> they came from Chicago, they had to have left
<u>very</u> early, like the night before. <u>Something urgent</u>
<u>to do</u>? What?

4 – BIG QUESTION! Why were these people going
to the T-Bone ranch?

Chewing on his pencil, Trey stared at the last thing he'd written and could not for the *life* of him think of how he was going to find the answer to that particular poser. He yawned and looked at his travelling clock on the bedside table: the glow-in-the-dark hands showed it was almost 11.30! Where had the time gone? He'd best turn his torch off and get to sleep, as in just seven hours' time, if he wasn't up and about, Gramps would be knocking on his door giving him the old "rise-and-shine-sonny-boy" routine and informing him, as he invariably did, that if the cows were up then he should be too.

Clicking off the torch, Trey lay back in the pitch darkness, thinking how different life was down here on the ranch from back home in Chicago. He'd been spending most of his summers down here since he didn't know when and it was his second home. Over the years he'd learned to shoot pretty good, skin a squirrel, ride a horse, rope a cow, climb trees, swim and a whole lot more. In fact this year Gramps had even taught him to drive, on the ranch's slightly battered Ford Model T. pick-up.

Now that he'd learned the basics he usually got some practice in by being the first person at the barn in the morning; after he'd loaded the back of the truck up with hay and a sack or two of grain he'd then drive it out to where the ranch's *remuda* of horses came in each morning to feed. It was a real incentive to get up early, and as he drifted off he wondered if that was why his gramps had taught him...

In his dream a woodpecker was outside the room where he was – and it sure must be a large one, the racket it was making. Then, from one instant to the next, Trey was awake and aware that the knocking was actually someone hammering at the front door of the ranch house. The luminous hands on his clock said that it was a quarter to five and still pitch-black. Now Trey could hear someone – sounded like the head ranch hand, Deacon Ames – shouting *"Boss!"* Something big had to be up, Trey thought to himself as he leaped out of bed and started for the stairs, but at least Mr. Ames wasn't yelling *"Fire!"*

"What's the matter?" he called out, halfway down the staircase; in the darkened hallway Trey could make out Deacon Ames, who had let himself in, and behind him he could hear Gramps's bedroom door opening.

"That you, Trey?"

"Yes, sir, Mr. Ames!"

"Git yer grandaddy, son, we got ourselves a situation."

"I hear him coming, Mr. Ames – what's happened?"

"Been a break-out in the north forty. Got at least a hundred head of cattle on the loose up there."

"How in tarnation they get out, Deke?"

Trey glanced behind him and saw Gramps appear in a shaft of moonlight at the top of the stairs in his slippers, hair dishevelled and still tying up the tasselled cord of his dressing gown.

"Abe Williams was out early and saw 'em. Said the fence was down, boss," said Deke. "He did the neighbourly thing and came by to tell me."

"But..." Trey moved aside to let his grandfather by.

"Weren't we out checking that run the other day, Gramps?"

"Sure were, son. Let me get my boots on, Deke, and I'll see you outside in five minutes..." Gramps turned to go back upstairs and stopped as he passed Trey. "You too, Trey, we're going to need every hand we have!"

Someone had lit a couple of oil lamps at the stables, but they created more shadows than useful light, so Trey had mostly saddled up Biscuit by touch. Luckily he'd done the job so often that it was almost second nature to him and he was ready to go right along with Deacon Ames, Gramps and the three other ranch hands.

It must've been twenty past six by the time they rode out into the still cold, still dark morning and there was at the very least a good half an hour or more before sunup. They were riding in pairs, a loose pack of half a dozen dogs excitedly running with them, and Trey was alongside Jimmy Tin, an 18-year-old, part-Cherokee boy, who had been with the Circle M for some six months now. He wasn't much of a conversationalist, but he could ride a horse better than anyone else Trey had *ever* seen. It was as if he could just think what he wanted them to do and they'd do it; he didn't even need reins, a saddle or spurs or anything.

Watching Jimmy with a horse, Gramps had said once, was like watching a virtuoso at work. Trey had had to look that particular word up, but having done so he had to agree with his grandfather: Jimmy Tin was a gen-u-ine genius.

They rode as fast as the time of day would let them, getting to the north forty just as the sun began to creep its pinky-orange fingers up over the horizon away to their right. Then they split up and spread out to look for the hundred or so cattle that were wandering off who knew where. It was, thought Trey as he spurred Biscuit into a gallop, going to be a long time till breakfast...

Everything belonged to someone in these parts. All of the great, rolling prairie was divided up somehow, either by the invisible county and state lines on maps, or by the actual, physical borders created by mile upon mile of barbed wire that separated ranch from ranch. And each ranch had a brand: a simple, recognizable design seared into the hide of every cow it owned so that, if an incident such as today's should occur, animals could be returned to their proper owner. The job now was to search out all the Circle M cows that had got themselves mixed up with cattle from the neighbouring

T-Bone ranch, separate them and bring them home. And as Trey knew, it was a task easier said than done.

As well as being an astonishing rider, Jimmy Tin could also read tracks like they were words on a page and he soon picked up a trail. Along with Blaze and Scratch, the two dogs that'd chosen to come with them, they set off in a vaguely westerly direction until they crested a hill to find themselves looking down a long, gentle slope to a large, natural waterhole. By now the sun was up, the chill was off the air and day had properly broken. In front of them, scattered around the deep bowl, were maybe fifty or sixty head of cattle, a lot of which were the russet-brown, horned Herefords the Circle M specialized in. Trey caught Jimmy's eye and they nodded at each other, one going left, the other right so that they could, with the dogs' help, bring all the animals together and then begin the job of weeding out theirs.

Trey and Biscuit had done this kind of work before, but he knew that Jimmy was the expert here, the one who should take the lead. His own job was to work with Blaze and Scratch to keep the Circle M cattle together, once Jimmy had successfully taken them out of the milling, lowing, increasingly agitated drove of animals. All was going very well until Trey saw Scratch lining himself up to nip the hocks of a skittery young calf, a bad habit he'd had since a puppy, and one even the ever-present threat of a kick in the noggin from the cows had failed to get him to drop.

"Scratch!" Trey yelled and whistled at the dog. "Back!"

But Trey's command came too late and Scratch launched his sneak attack. Separated from its mother, the calf panicked, rolling its eyes and mooing loudly and plaintively. Wheeling Biscuit around to go over and sort out Scratch, Trey and his mount were both taken by surprise when the calf's mother unexpectedly lurched into action right next to them.

From being in complete control, Trey's world went into a spin as Biscuit reared unexpectedly, violently jerking him out of his saddle and making him lose his right stirrup. In an effort to stop himself being thrown, Trey instinctively grabbed for Biscuit's mane, dropped the split reins as he did so, and found himself clinging awkwardly to the horse's neck. But worse, *much* worse, his left foot was now slowly slipping out of its stirrup, making it next to impossible for him to boost himself back up!

Trey knew that if he didn't do something, and do it quick, he would find himself flat on the ground and in danger of being trampled on by the jittery cattle now stomping and shoving all around him. And the likelihood of being able to get up and walk away if *that* happened was not good.

Almost as bad was the possibility that Jimmy Tin would see him messing up; he did *not* want that. And it was this thought that gave him the idea. He'd seen Jimmy get himself up onto a trotting and unsaddled horse just using its mane, and, as far as Trey could see, attempting this trick himself was his one and only chance.

Taking a deep breath, Trey allowed his boot to slip out of the left stirrup – there was ab-so-*lute*-ly no going back now – and let both his legs swing down in an arc towards the ground as he hung onto a nervous Biscuit's burr-encrusted mane for dear life. He knew he'd only have one chance to bend his knees and spring back up the moment they hit the ground, like he'd seen Jimmy Tin do. If he messed up, he thought as his feet hit the ground, he'd had it...

It took a moment or two for Trey to take in that he'd actually made it, a feeling of intense relief surging through him; then, quickly settling himself, he leaned forward, patting the horse's sweat-covered neck. "It's over, Biscuit..."

"Everything okay?"

Trey looked round to see Jimmy Tin galloping his way and he smiled and waved, inwardly cursing that

Jimmy must've seen the whole incident. "Yup!" he called back.

"You did good." Jimmy pulled his horse up next to Biscuit, leaned over, grabbed the dangling reins and handed them over to Trey. "Nice piece of riding there. Only a few more to cut out. Be done soon."

Trey watched Jimmy canter away, shaking his head in amazement. He had *never* heard Jimmy praise anyone's riding before. Ever. As he watched him manoeuvring the last Circle M cows out of the mixed-up herd, he patted Biscuit again. "We did good!"

Ten minutes later they were driving the reclaimed animals back towards the pasture they'd escaped from during the night, cutting across some T-Bone land to make the journey shorter. They weren't far from their destination when a young, feisty bull cut loose from the back of the herd and made a break for it, heading for a nearby stand of trees.

"He's mine!" Trey yelled, urging Biscuit into a gallop and taking off in hot pursuit, Blaze running with him; he knew he was showing off, but there was part of him that wanted to prove he was good at riding, as well as not falling off.

Rather than follow the animal through the trees,

Trey skirted round them and headed it off, sending the dog to return it to the herd. As he was about to ride back a flash of white caught his eye and he looked down the hillside where the T-Bone spread nestled in the valley below. It didn't take him long to see where the glint of light had come from – a big white automobile, under some live oaks way out back of the ranch house. A big white, brand-new Buick Monarch, if he wasn't very much mistaken. But what was it doing parked up like that? It made you think that they didn't want anyone who happened to come visiting to see it was there. Leastways, he was sure that's what Trent Gripp would think.

As he gently urged Biscuit into a trot, Trey puzzled over what he'd just seen and what it could mean. It was, he reckoned, highly unlikely that there was a *second* white Buick Monarch in the neighbourhood, so the men he'd seen yesterday had not only called in on Bowyer Dunne – the man who owned the T-Bone ranch – they'd stayed over.

Trey knew that Gramps and Mr. Dunne were not on what anyone would call "friendly terms". Gramps really did not like the man at all, but Trey had never heard him refer to his neighbour as a gangster. Last time Trey had been around when Dunne's name was mentioned, Gramps had called him a "low-down, no-good snake-in-the-grass", and then apologized for his language to Gramma Cecilia.

This, thought Trey as he rejoined Jimmy Tin, definitely came under the heading of "interesting"...

4 CURIOUSER...

It was late on that same day when the telephone rang in the study, loud in the now-silent house. Gramps, who had fallen asleep by his desk, jerked awake and grabbed the receiver on the second ring.

"That you, Bob?" he said, stifling a yawn.

"Who else you expecting to call you back at this time of night, Ace – Mae West?"

"Hope springs eternal!" said Gramps, smiling at the thought of the "blonde bombshell" actress.

"They do say... So, don't keep me in suspense,

why'd you leave a message for me to get in touch, pronto?"

"Got some more information about the Buick with the Illinois plates."

"What'd you find out?"

"Trey saw the car again." Gramps took a sip of the brandy he'd brought with him to the study while he waited for Bob Bonner to return his call.

"At the T-Bone?"

"Yup. Parked where it wouldn't ordinarily be seen, out behind Bowyer Dunne's place."

There was a fairly long, crackly silence. "He sure?"

"*I'm* sure, Bob. Took a quiet ride up there myself and checked."

"Interesting. That Dunne, he's something big in the local Republican party, right?"

"Not local, Bob. He's treasurer for the whole midwest area; and, I am reliably informed, this includes Chicago."

"Which begs the question: what is such a fine and upstanding type like Bowyer Dunne doing getting all hugger-mugger with a bunch of lowlifes?"

"And in an election year, no less."

"As you say, Ace, in an election year..."

* * *

Upstairs, Trey lay in bed, having been jolted awake by the two short rings of the telephone; he'd tried real hard to stop himself falling asleep, but considering he'd been up since way before dawn – and on the go ever since – it wasn't surprising he'd dozed off. He sat up, wondering who it was at the other end of the line. He'd kind of been expecting the call, as earlier in the evening he'd happened to be going by Gramps's study and, what with the door being ajar and all, couldn't help but overhear him talking to someone and asking them "to get Bob to call back, as soon as possible, if not sooner". He'd sounded *very* emphatic. Like it was extremely important.

Who was this Bob character? And what could be so vital that Gramps *had* to talk to him?

Trey didn't dare get out of bed to see if he could hear what was being said as the stairs creaked wildly, no matter how hard you tried to tiptoe, and he did *not* want to be caught in the act. Instead, he checked his travel clock and saw that it was 11.45. Very nearly tomorrow.

He thought about getting his torch out, but decided not to (you never knew when you were really going to need a torch, so there was no point in wasting the batteries when you could think perfectly well in the dark). Lying there in the pitch-black, Trey ran over in his head all the things that had happened since Deacon

Ames had turned up with the news of the break-out in the north forty.

During the day there had been a couple of other events that were noteworthy enough for Trey to have actually made a note of them. The first had been the astonishing news that the cattle hadn't gotten out because a fence had broke! Trey had gone to see the evidence with his own eyes, and not one of the triple-stranded lines of barbed wire had shown *any* sign at all of rust or age, and *every* sign of having been sliced with wire cutters. Gramps had been beside himself, kicking a fence post so hard that he'd hurt his foot.

Trey had asked him if it was rustlers, to which he'd got the unusually grumpy reply of "No, son, it was barbarian, hooligan saboteurs!", which, to be honest, didn't seem likely in Kansas. The big question was, if it wasn't rustlers or barbarian saboteurs, who would've deliberately let the cows out? Even though he wanted to carry on talking about the subject he could tell that Gramps really was not in the mood, so he left it for a bit; then, when they were at the tack shed, fixing up some of the older saddles, he asked Jimmy Tin.

Jimmy had stated that it wasn't his place to say too much, but that there had been a number of other incidents which The Boss (i.e. Gramps) was of the opinion were down to the folks over at the T-Bone. He would not be drawn on *which* folks, or what these "incidents" were.

And then there was the sighting of the white Buick Monarch at the T-Bone ranch, which Trey had thought really was a piece of headline news. But, once again, there had been an almost complete lack of reaction from Gramps when he'd told him about it.

And that, as far as Trey knew, was it; nothing else remotely interesting had happened in the last few days, so had Gramps called this man Bob because of the gangsters, or was it the possible sabotage? Like Austin J. Randall said in *Chapter 5 – Deduction*: "When you have eliminated the impossible, whatever remains, *however improbable*, must be the truth". This piece of advice, Trey had thought, was so important that he'd copied it out and put it at the front of his notebook, as a constant reminder of the kind of thinking he had to emulate from now on.

From his point of view, the likelihood of there being "barbarian, hooligan saboteurs" in the area was both pretty impossible, and fairly improbable. Which therefore left the gangsters as the reason for the phone call to this Bob. And the need to speak to him so urgently. Because why were gangsters visiting a man Trey knew his gramps thought was an absolute pill?

His eyelids beginning to droop, Trey wondered

what his favourite private eye, Trent "Pistol" Gripp ("The man with the itchiest trigger finger in New York City", according to *Black Ace* magazine), would do... After checking he had a full clip in his trusty Colt .45 automatic, he'd more than likely melt into the shadows and, using his custom lock-picks if he had to, get into the T-Bone ranch house and snoop around to see what he could find. Some hope *he* had of being able to do that, Trey had to admit. Even if he owned a set of lock-picks, Austin J. Randall had so far omitted to instruct his readers on how to use them.

Gramps had laid the law down in no uncertain terms that the T-Bone ranch was totally off-limits. If he ever found out Trey had been anywhere *near* the place, Gramps would have a conniption fit. Even so, Trey was going to *have* to find some way of getting a closer look. There were things going on there he didn't know nearly enough about...

5 AS LUCK WOULD HAVE IT

It was, Trey thought later, extremely odd how things had a way of working out sometimes. The very next day he was with Wolf Baxter, one of the friends he'd made over the years he'd been coming down to Topeka – Mr. Baxter owned the feed store and gas station nearest to the Circle M, which was how him and Wolf had met. The two of them had been over behind one of the barns, generally wasting time in one of the best ways they knew how – catapulting pebbles at old tin cans – when Wolf casually mentioned that he'd heard there was a birthday party at the T-Bone ranch that afternoon.

"Say what?" Trey queried. "Whose? I didn't know Mr. Dunne had kids."

"Don't think he does." Wolf fired a devastating shot which spanged a can spectacularly up into the air. "My ma was talking at breakfast. Something about Mr. Dunne having a nephew from New Orleans, or New York, or New Jersey – or maybe even New *Hamp*shire for all *I* know. Anyway, wherever he's from, he's staying, and it's his birthday and they're inviting people from round here – y'know, kids – so's there'll be someone his age there. You get yours?"

"My what?"

"Invitation, fella."

Trey shook his head, then loosed off a pebble that somehow managed to knock two cans off the fence. "*I* won't get an invitation, bud. Not me..."

"Why the heck not?'

"My gramps and Mr. Dunne? They do *not* see eye to eye." Trey kicked the dirt around, looking for some more ammunition. "How about you bring me a piece of cake?"

"Not me, bud..." Wolf pulled the elastic back as far as he could and aimed. "*I'm* not going."

Trey watched a particularly rusty can disintegrate

as Wolf's shot smacked it dead centre. "Huh? You're not – why?"

"Some goofy party, for some big city jingle-brain? I got better things to do."

"Right, but..."

"But what?" Wolf rummaged in his jeans pockets for another pebble.

"Nothing..." Trey loaded up his catapult and beat Wolf to the last can with a zingingly accurate shot. He'd had an idea and it was a humdinger...

And so that was how, after lunch, Trey got to be riding away on Biscuit, ostensibly to visit Wolf at his place, but really going off on a mission to the party at the T-Bone ranch.

He did feel a *tiny* bit bad about ignoring his grandfather's stated wishes not to go near the T-Bone ranch. But it had occurred to him that if he *did* manage to find out anything useful – about the gangsters, or who at the T-Bone was responsible for the "incidents" – then he was pretty sure Gramps would forgive him. And if he didn't get any info, then Gramps need never know; "What the eyes don't see," as he was known to say, "the heart won't grieve over."

Slung over Trey's shoulder was the Kodak No. 2C

Autographic Jnr camera he'd gotten for Christmas. It was folded snugly in its leatherette cover and now travelled with him most everywhere he went, just in case. Thus far, Trey had to admit, he had yet to find a "just in case" moment, but he knew he would be prepared if and when he ever did.

Riding along, Trey fell to thinking about what it would be like to have a *real* mystery, imagining himself involved – right up to his neck, like Trent Gripp would get – in the action. Then he shook his head at how stupid he was being, as he *had* a case. He had to find out who the men in the white Buick Monarch were!

He started to think about the T-Bone party because *that* was his humdinger of an idea...he was going to walk right in, and if asked who he was tell them "Wolf Baxter". They both had the same colour hair, and were pretty much the same size, and he was sure no one at the ranch, especially its owner, would know one way or the other that he wasn't telling the truth.

Trey kicked Biscuit into a gallop and they stormed off down the dirt road, leaving a cloud of dust behind them.

Unfortunately, getting into the party did not turn out to be as much of a breeze as Trey had hoped. His idea of pretending to be Wolf went straight out the window the moment he saw that it looked like there were people checking invitations at the main entrance.

Riding past, as if he was on the way somewhere else entirely, Trey glimpsed activity at the end of the gravel drive that led to the T-Bone ranch house and put his mind to thinking how the heck he was going to get himself up there. Then he noticed that the side of the road bordering on to T-Bone land was effectively fenced off by thick brush and cottonwood trees, stopping him from seeing in...but then again, presumably stopping anyone else seeing out.

Trey carried on riding until he found a place where he felt it would be safe to tie up Biscuit, while he was off on his mission. Checking that there was no one around, Trey went back down the road towards the ranch's entrance and then, thinking to himself that it was now or never, took the bull by the horns and snuck into the undergrowth.

Keeping low, and as quiet as possible, he made his way through the vegetation to the point where he could see out the other side, then stopped to take stock of his situation. He'd read about people doing that in quite a few stories and now, here on his own and about to break cover, it seemed like a pretty good idea. He moved out of the brush and, as he went to stand behind one of the larger cottonwood trees, he noticed something on the ground in the leaf fall. Something that was so well camouflaged he'd almost overlooked it.

"Copperhead..." he whispered, stopping dead in his tracks. He recognized the pattern, the skin of one of these poisonous snakes having been nailed up on the wall of the feed barn by Deacon Ames. What had he been told about this snake? Apart from that they were poisonous? Trey thought hard and fast, recalling that Mr. Ames had said you'd be in a deal more trouble if it was a cottonmouth you were staring at.

The snake hadn't moved an inch, and Trey remembered Mr. Ames saying that, "by and large", copperheads preferred to avoid trouble and froze where they were if disturbed. Hoping that Mr. Ames knew what he was talking about, Trey shuffled sideways then ran for it at full pelt, right into the open. As he burst out of the trees he almost collided with someone.

"Whoa!" The man, dressed in work clothes, was likely a T-Bone hand. He made something of a show of being taken by surprise. "You're going like a bullet from a gun there, boy. What ya doing out here anyhow?"

"Um...I, ah..." For a second Trey was at a complete loss, as the reality of having almost stepped on a venomous snake sank in. "I was...I was, you know, exploring..." He waved his arms about. "And then I needed...well put it like this, I had a whatchamacallit, call of nature, so I went..." Trey jerked a thumb behind him at the trees, cursing himself for making such a *dumb* excuse.

"That so?" The man looked Trey up and down, then shrugged and walked away. "Next time I suggest you use the facilities up at the house, son. We call it Copperhead Alley in there, coulda got yourself bit..."

Trey watched the man go, astonished that he'd managed to survive not only an encounter with a snake, but also being discovered sneaking into the party. Someone must be looking out for him, as his gramps always said when he got an unexpected piece of good luck.

With one last glance behind him, Trey made his way up to the house, only to find the party was being held *al fresco*, spread out across the ranch's extensive property. This left him somewhat nonplussed as it meant he was going to have absolutely no opportunity to go snooping round the house. Which had been another part of his plan.

According to *How to Become a Private Eye in 10 Easy Lessons – Chapter 7 – Preparations,* conducting a thorough investigation of your target area was of paramount importance to a mission. But now it looked like all the strategies and schemes he'd come up with (especially the one about secretly photographing the important documents Bowyer Dunne was *sure* to have left on his desk) were dead in the water.

The "target area" now turned out to be a large grassy expanse on which the owner, Bowyer Dunne, had gone to quite some expense to create a kind of rodeo theme for his nephew, right down to having dressed himself up in a checked shirt, heavily tooled boots, silver-decorated leather chaps and a wide-brimmed Stetson. He looked, in Trey's opinion, like a kid who'd just walked out of a store wearing every single one of his new purchases; and while a kid might just get away with it, Bowyer Dunne simply looked ridiculous.

There were sideshows and amusements, like at a carney, and a big pit where a whole pig was being roasted on a spit, and people were also making hot dogs and hamburgers, in case you couldn't wait for the main attraction. Elsewhere a couple of the T-Bone cowhands were giving demonstrations of lassoing and bareback riding, but this stuff was only of interest to the city-slicker visitors – of whom there were quite a few; the men in their suits, the woman in bright frocks.

But no matter where he looked Trey could see neither hide nor hair of the four men he'd encountered out on the back road. The thing was, now he was *at* the party and on the lookout for things – and people – to photograph, it occurred to him that some of those people might not *want* to have a camera pointed at them. With this thought in mind Trey kept the Kodak in its case and tried to make himself as inconspicuous as possible.

But after ten minutes of traipsing around, and only some cotton candy to show for his troubles, Trey decided he had to get serious, stop pussyfooting around and take some risks. Because, if he didn't start taking some pictures there'd be nothing to put in the file. Once he started a file. He hadn't gotten around to that yet, but he would, because Austin J. Randall was insistent that you should have one for every case you were working on. And while it was true that he didn't have a client, he was going to treat *The Mystery of the White Limousine* – as the story would surely be called if it was in *Black Ace* magazine – exactly as if it was a piece of real detective business.

But the moment he set to work he got the very strong feeling that *he* was the one being watched – which made him feel decidedly twitchy. What if it was the man he now thought of as "Bad Frank" eyeballing him? It didn't help matters that he only just avoided being introduced to the birthday boy (what a flat tyre *he* looked). Then some woman with enough make-up on for two people grabbed him and tried to rope him into "join a team and play a game!" *As if,* he'd thought as he made his escape.

In the end it was his own caution that got the better of him.

He was so busy checking this way and that to see if anyone was watching him that he got careless about looking where he was going and walked right into a group of people standing around chatting.

"Oh, sorry...excuse me...beg your pardon, ma'am, sir...people..." Trey felt himself blush as he attempted to apologize, at the same time as back his way out.

"Oh look, he has a *camera!*" A woman pointed at Trey. "Smile, everyone!"

Six people turned on a dime to stare at Trey expectantly, with fixed grins slapped on their faces. At which point he had no choice in the matter: he *had* to take a picture. And it was there and then, as he stared into the viewfinder trying to frame the shot, that he noticed one of the men looked familiar. Staring back at him was a pale-complexioned guy with heavy tortoiseshell glasses. He finally clicked who it was as he checked the film had been wound on. It was the third suit who'd been out on the North Road, the one he hadn't really paid much attention to!

Trey almost froze – would the man recognize him? If you were trying to do a job "undercover" it was probably best not to make an exhibition of yourself. Like being dragged in to take pictures. But it was too late now, he had to carry on as if nothing had happened.

"Smile, please!" Trey said, keeping his head firmly down, praying the man would not recollect that he'd seen him before, and pinning his hopes on the fact that he was a great deal tidier and a whole lot better dressed than when they'd last met. He pressed the shutter as they all crowed "Cheese!" in unison.

The picture taken, Trey was about to dash off and get himself as elsewhere as possible (if he'd ever had any doubts that the detective business required nerves of steel and a cast-iron gut, the last couple of minutes had certainly dispelled them), when his attention was caught by the sight of a magnificent, royal blue car – it looked like a Duesenberg – coming up the drive. He'd never seen one of these cars in the flesh before and, this being far too good an opportunity to miss, he moved to where he would get the best picture. As the auto swept to a halt (a beautiful, two-seater boat-tail coupé with scarlet coach lines, red leather interior and the top down, he noted), Trey squinted into his viewfinder and got the shot all lined up.

Exactly at the moment he was about to press the shutter release, the man driving got out, and so did his female companion. Trey couldn't help but stare at the woman, who looked like a million dollars, dripping jewels and swathed in yards of ruby-red silky material that matched both her lipstick and her shoes. Her shiny dark brown hair was cut short in the very latest style, which he'd heard his mother refer to a tad scornfully as "boyish", although it had to be said *he'd* never seen a boy look anything like this lady.

Bowyer Dunne rushed to greet them; he'd taken off his Stetson – revealing a shock of bright, coppery-red hair – and was waving the hat in the air as he strode forward.

"Howdy, Mario!" Bowyer Dunne thrust a hand out as he eyeballed the woman. "And this must be?"

"My secretary..." The guy called Mario winked as he slapped Bowyer Dunne on the back. "How you doing, cowboy?"

And *klick!* went the shutter.

Immediately, Bowyer Dunne turned and stared straight at him, a frown creasing his face.

"Hey, kid!" he said.

Trey's immediate thought was to hightail it pretty darn quick in the opposite direction and lose himself in the crowds, but a calmer voice told him that whatever he did he should do it slowly. Running would just make him look guilty. Before he could make a move Trey saw the man called Mario grab Bowyer Dunne by the shoulder.

"Hey, cowboy! How's about getting us all to a *bar*?" he said in a very fake "western" accent. "Feels like we've been breathing dust ever since we crossed the state line!"

Right then a gaggle of people appeared to greet Mario and his companion, surrounding them and Bowyer Dunne, and sweeping all of them away in the direction of the house. Trey stayed where he was and breathed a somewhat large sigh of relief. That had been close.

Although he knew he should probably make himself scarce, the car was such a beauty he couldn't leave without taking a closer look. Walking up to the Duesenberg, Trey tentatively reached out to touch one of the massive, gracefully sweeping front mudguards.

"A *real* doozy of a Duesey, huh, kid?"

Trey cursed his stupidity for not getting away while the going was good.

"Sure is, mister," he said as brightly as he could, looking round at the man standing behind him. "It's a Model X, right?"

"On the button, kid, you know your automobiles." The man smiled as he went over to the car and posed with one foot on the chrome running board, smoothing back his slicked hair with both hands. "This'll give you a great snap – and do an extra print, why doncha! Give it to Mr. Dunne to send on to me."

"Okay..." Trey checked the back of the Kodak, saw that he only had a couple of shots left and frowned, "...but..."

"There's a fin in it for you," the man said, a five-dollar bill in his right hand. "Nothing for nothing in this man's world, right?"

"Okay, mister..." Five dollars, Trey thought as he framed the picture and pressed the shutter, was he serious? You could get a whole *roll* of pictures taken for that, *and* have a chunk of change.

"Thanks, kid, give it to Mr. Dunne," the man said as he handed over the crisp new note. "Tell him it's for Tony Burrell, that's two 'r's and two 'l's, kid – and he'll know where to get me."

Trey found himself looking at the bill. He knew he couldn't accept it, as how was he ever going to get a print to this man? But before he could give it back the guy had disappeared. This had, Trey thought, been quite some afternoon, what with one thing and another. Putting the money in his pocket he was looking to see if there was anything else he should try and get one last shot of, when he saw Mr. Shirtsleeves, the man who'd been changing the Buick's tyre out on the North Road. Trey turned right round, took a deep breath, and began to walk – not run, he was *not* going to run – in the opposite direction.

It was absolutely, definitely time to leave the party. Which, as he planned to go via the main gate, should be a heck of a lot easier than getting in…

"Did you see that kid, Joe?" Bowyer Dunne was standing by the window of his office.

Joe Cullen shrugged. "What kid?"

"The kid with the camera!" Bowyer lifted a slat of the Venetian blind and glanced out of the window. "I think he was taking pictures."

"And?"

Dunne turned round, scowling.

"And? I'll tell you what the 'and' is – there's a possibility he could have one of me and Mario…" Bowyer Dunne took a white linen handkerchief out of his pocket and dabbed perspiration off his top lip. "You *sure* you didn't see this boy?"

Joe shook his head. "It's a big party, quite a few boys running round out there." He watched his boss, who was now chewing a fingernail. "The kid probably just got given a new snapper, boss, any pictures he takes'll be out of focus and all the heads cut off."

"But they might not! This is an *election* year, in case you hadn't noticed, Joe, and I have a position of some influence in the Republican party. While both Mario and

I might agree in private that keeping the Prohibition laws exactly as they are is a good idea, a picture of me with a Chicago crime boss is a risk I can't take!" Bowyer Dunne thumped his fist on the desk. "What in the world is anyone doing giving a *kid* a camera? Who wants them taking pictures all over the place – snap, snap, snap!"

Waiting for his boss's rant to finish, Joe Cullen got out his pack of Chesterfields and shook a cigarette up. This, he thought as he struck a match, could take some time.

"I pay you to just stand around and smoke, Joe?"

Joe's hand stopped an inch or two from the tip of the cigarette he was about to light; he looked at his boss, then blew out the match. "No."

"Damn straight. So go ask around, okay? Find out who the kid is."

"And then?"

"I have to tell you *every*thing?" Bowyer sat down behind his desk, hunching forward and jabbing an accusatory finger. "You get the film off of him and bring it back to me. And make completely darn sure Mario doesn't get wind of this, or my life will not be worth living, I can tell you that for nothing. I make myself clear?"

Joe knew that Mario Andrusa was a tricky customer, and one with a hair-trigger temper, but why he would kick up a fuss about being in a snapshot with the likes of Bowyer Dunne was not at *all* clear. "Yes, Mr. Dunne, you do."

"Terrific. Now go…"

6 TUESDAY, SEPTEMBER 4TH, CHICAGO

Trey stood on the sidewalk, looking up and down the street. All the signs that fall was approaching were there if you cared to look for them. As Austin J. Randall said, in almost every chapter of *How to Become a Private Eye in 10 Easy Lessons*, it was the smallest detail that could often break a case and so it was essential to practise looking at things. Anything would do, according to Mr. Randall, just so long as you looked at it *very* hard and remembered *everything* you could.

A quick glance at his watch told Trey that he'd better

make tracks into school, rather than mooch around outside, because if there was one thing the Mount Vernon Academy demanded of its students it was punctuality. He couldn't believe summer was well and truly over (which, as Monday had been Labour Day, it surely was) and that he was unlikely to be visiting the Circle M again for a good six months.

His parents had arrived to collect him a couple of days after Bowyer Dunne's party at the T-Bone ranch, and as they drove away Trey had waved goodbye to Gramps, Gramma Cecilia and any chance of solving *The Mystery of the White Limousine*. He shrugged at the thought, and was about to join some other boys on their way into the Academy's grounds, when a big Packard drew up. The chauffeur jumped out and opened the rear door with a smart salute.

This was not such an unusual sight, but Trey hung back and watched anyway, noting the auto's special two-tone, dove grey and black paint finish. A pallid dark-haired boy, probably about the same age as Trey, got out of the car and nervously looked around, pushing his gold, wire-framed spectacles up his nose. A swot, if ever he'd seen one, in Trey's opinion. The boy was about to walk off when someone inside the car called out – it sounded like the name "Alex".

As he turned to go, Trey saw a man, also wearing

glasses, get out of the Packard. He was holding what looked like books that the boy had forgotten, and Trey stopped as if someone had stepped on his brakes. He might not have a clue who the boy was, but he ab-so-*lute*-ly, no doubt about it, one *hundred* per cent recognized this person – it was the man with the tortoiseshell spectacle frames Trey had first seen, along with Bad Frank and Tall Suit, when their white Buick Monarch had gotten a flat out on the North Road. *And* who had been in the group of people Trey'd had to photograph at the T-Bone ranch party!

Case reopened!

School was *not* the easiest of places to act like a detective in search of facts. To start with, you were in class most of the time, and when you weren't you were supposed to be en route to the next one. Then there were all the people always on the lookout to catch you *not* doing whatever it was you were supposed to be doing.

By the end of the day Trey had discovered that Alex's surname was Little and that he was, like himself, in Seventh Grade. The information had been duly recorded in his trusty notebook. It was not, Trey had to admit, a lot to show for a day's work, but, along with Latin, Geography, double Math, English and Music, there hadn't been a whole lot of time left over for sleuthing. Still, he thought on the walk home, it was a start and better than nothing.

After dinner – and with the next day's History report finally completed – Trey was still at his desk. He was sitting in the pool of light thrown by the black gooseneck lamp his father had brought back from the office for him, pensively chewing on a pencil. He knew he had to get down to rubbing a few brain cells together to create some heat, as Trent Gripp would say, so he could figure out what to do next.

On the pad in front of him he'd written down some notes, but once again they didn't amount to much. All he knew for *certain* was that Bowyer Dunne had played host to some people who Trey was pretty sure were gangsters. Especially the one called Frank. He was *very* sure about him. And one of these people, a Mr. Little as he'd discovered, had a son just started at the Mount Vernon Academy. Added to which there was the Mario character with the Duesenberg; although Trey had no idea who he was, he looked very much like he was the kind of guy to end up with his mug on the front page of the papers – and for all the wrong reasons. And to be honest, Trey didn't know what to make of Mr. Tony Burrell, the man who'd paid him five dollars for a single snapshot.

Trey sat bolt upright. The film! What with one thing and another (mainly schoolwork, it had to be said in his defence) he hadn't gotten round to developing it yet. For all he knew it could be stuffed full of clues! He stood up, ready to make straight for his bathroom, where his pop had helped him turn a corner into a simple but effective darkroom, but as he pushed his sleeves back he noticed the time. Any minute now someone would be by to make sure he was getting ready for bed. He slumped down in his chair. This job was just going to have to wait.

Trey scribbled *"DEVELOP FILM!!!"* on his notepad, underlined it three times, then sat back shaking his head and examining the tooth-marks on the end of his pencil. The more he thought about it, the more it was obvious that *something* was very definitely up in Topeka. But there were, he knew, always two sides to every story and there was always the possibility he could be wrong. What if these suspicious visitors to the T-Bone ranch had nothing at all to do with the sabotage at the Circle M? But if they did, would that mean that Gramps was involved in the same kind of business as types like Bad Frank and the Mario guy?

"*Not* possible..." Trey muttered to himself, frowning as he recalled the mystery phone call to the person called Bill. "Not in a *million* years..."

No matter which way he looked at it, there was only one path open to him: if he wanted to find out anything about anything he was going to have to bite the bullet and talk to sappy Alex Little. This would, he knew, be something of a strain as all they had in common in the whole world was being Seventh Graders, which was no great start for a friendship of any type.

Austin J. Randall made it quite clear that one of the main attributes anyone wishing to enter the detective business had to develop was the ability to successfully pretend to be someone you were not. Well, Trey thought, here was his chance to put theory into practice.

7 WEDNESDAY, SEPTEMBER 5TH, TOPEKA

"**W**hat?!" Bowyer Dunne yelled; leaping up as if he'd sat on a fistful of thumbtacks, he sent his heavy oak and leather office chair flying across the room on its castors. Then he leaned forward, his knuckles on the burnished walnut desk, glowering. "*Who* did you say the kid with the camera was?"

"Old man MacIntyre's grandson, Mr. Dunne," said Joe Cullen, making a "who'da-thought-it" face and staying right where he was by the office door.

"Old man MacIntyre's *grand*son...that little weevil

wasn't even *invited* to the darn party!" Bowyer Dunne's face reddened to match his hair as he pointed a stubby finger at the man who currently held the position of Head of Security at Dunne Inc. "This is *terrible*! And how come it's taken you *three whole weeks* – count them, Joe – to find out that the kid is Ace MacIntyre's grandson?"

Joe wanted to say that he had rather more important things to do than chase down some kid who may, or may not, have some blurred snapshots in his possession. But he didn't. "There was no list of who came, boss, and then school went back and—"

"No list?" interrupted Bowyer. "*Why* was there no list, for crying out loud?"

"Well, y'see, boss..."

"What? Spit it out, man."

"*Mrs.* Dunne was the one got the kids to come. I had nothing to do with that side of things." Joe shifted from one foot to the other. "And, like I say, there was no list made, just invitations mailed. Apparently. That's what Mrs. Dunne told me."

"She did, did she?" Bowyer grabbed his chair, pulled it back and sat down with a grunt of frustration. "Right, well, fine...*fine* – but, but, but what was MacIntyre's grandson doing at *my* party taking pictures? Huh? What? And how'd he get in? They were checking invitations at the gate and he sure as heck did *not* have one. So how'd he get in?!"

Joe shrugged, frankly at a loss what to say.

"Well he got in *some*how!" Bowyer carried on regardless. "And I am in *so* much trouble now – we have *got* to get that film, Joe, and then tear it up or burn it or whatever we have to do to destroy it!"

"Right, boss." Joe was beginning to wonder if Mr. Dunne had gone off his nut, the way he was acting.

"I cannot *believe* he sent a *spy*!" Bowyer got up and went to stare out of his second-floor office window at downtown Topeka.

"Who?" Joe asked, finding it difficult to follow the way the conversation was going.

Bowyer turned round. "MacIntyre, you idiot! It's obvious *he* put the kid up to it...he must've found out about the meeting, somehow, and sent that boy in like some undercover Bureau cop! You believe that? His own flesh and blood? It's despicable!"

"But—"

"And whaddaya know? The kid swans right in like he owns the place, takes a bunch of pictures – including one of me with Mario – then walks right out again, five bucks up on the whole deal according to Tony Burrell! Could've been in the house, for all we know!"

"No, I don't think—"

"So I *have* to have that film back! For one thing, MacIntyre would just *love* to get a picture of me, the Chairman of the Republican party's Mid-West Fundraising Committee – dressed as a cowboy, no less – with Mario Andrusa, a man known as 'Missouri's Mr. Mob'!" Bowyer Dunne made quotation marks in the air with his fingers. "He has put many *thousands* of dollars into our campaign to help ensure we get Herbert Hoover elected this November, and we all know every cent of it is bootleg booze money, plain and simple."

"The man in the street doesn't like Prohibition, boss."

"That still doesn't make it legal."

Bowyer sat back down again and Joe watched silently as the man ran his fingers distractedly through his thatch of red hair. Joe had advised his boss against having the birthday party the same day as the big meeting, but had been overruled, told in no uncertain terms that the shindig would be, to quote, "excellent cover" should anyone wonder why there were so many automobiles at the ranch. Right, that was going to work, especially when those autos included a certain bright blue, very noticeable Duesenberg. But Joe was in no doubt that this was *not* the time to remind his boss – never a man to take kindly to being proved wrong – at whose feet the fault lay.

"Don't you think we'd know if MacIntyre had the pictures, boss? Wouldn't he have done something with them by now, if he was gonna?"

"There's still two months to go before the election, and are you forgetting the man's a lifelong Democrat, and a big donor to their campaign? He's waiting for the right moment to do the most damage, Joe, *that's* what *he's* doing! Don't you get it?"

"Thing is, boss, from what I managed to dig up on the boy, he's a keen snapper. And right now, he's back in Chicago, along with his camera, and something tells me the film also."

"Oh really, Joe?" Bowyer sneered. "And exactly *why* do you think that…exactly what *proof* do you have?"

"If Ace MacIntyre was gonna make use of what was on that film he'd have had to develop it first, boss. Otherwise, how would he know if what was on it was going to be any use to him? And…" Joe got a small leather-bound notebook out of his jacket pocket and opened it, "…as far as I can tell neither he, nor his good lady wife, has taken a film into any of the local pharmacies or stores specializing in photographic whatnotery in the last three weeks. And I have been all *over* Topeka. I think the boy took it back home with him, Mr. Dunne."

Bowyer's right eyelid twitched as he sat, staring into

the middle distance and tried to work out if this was good news, or bad news.

"This is good news, Mr. Dunne," said Joe, inadvertently echoing his boss's thoughts. "The kid develops it, he won't know who anyone is."

"*He* may not, but what if he shows the pictures to his father? Thought about *that*, Joe? And even if the film is in Chicago, like you say," Bowyer stood up again, pointing to himself with both index fingers, "*I* still need it back. Tony Burrell told Mario about the kid taking his picture and he's been hounding me…"

"Mario?" Joe frowned. "Why's *he* so fired up about these pictures, boss?"

"First off, he's more than a little annoyed I didn't personally tell him there was a chance we'd been snapped together."

"But surely *he* ain't the one going to be in trouble if those snaps ever get out."

"So much *you* know…" Bowyer Dunne sat back in his chair. "You ever meet *Mrs.* Andrusa?"

"No, why?"

"As it happens, she's the beloved only child of the one man can tell Mario what to do; he's what I'm reliably informed is called *Capo di tutti Capi*, something like that – 'The Boss of Bosses', a real big cheese." Bowyer sat back down. "She's a very nice woman, I am sure,

Mrs. Andrusa, but I gather not blessed in the looks department. Unlike Mario's 'secretary'. You recall her, Joe?"

"Sure do."

"She was in those pictures too, Joe, and were Mario's father-in-law to see them…well, let me put it this way: *if* he does, Mario's a dead man." Bowyer neatened up an already very tidy desk. "Leastways that's what Mario told me, which is the reason why he's so 'fired up', as you put it."

"Okay, I see…"

"No, no you don't." The colour drained from Bowyer's face.

"You okay, boss?"

"I…" Bowyer looked like a cushion that'd just been sat on by Fatty Arbuckle. "Look, I only said it because Mario was shouting at me down the phone and making all kinds of threats I happen to know he's very capable of seeing come true…"

Joe waited, but Bowyer remained silent. "What did you say, boss?"

"I told Mario I already *had* the film…and that I'd gotten rid of it."

"What?"

"I know, I know – like I already said, he was shouting at me. And since you found out who *actually* has the

68

pictures, it's even worse!" Bowyer sat up and squared his shoulders, like he was trying to throw off all his feelings of dejection and failure. "So there's only one thing for it."

"There is?"

"Yes," Bowyer leaned forward. "You are going to catch the next train to Chicago... I don't care how much it costs, or what you have to do, Joe – I do *not* care – just get that film back!"

8 THURSDAY, SEPTEMBER 6TH, CHICAGO

It had been almost *too* easy to become pals with Alex Little. The kid was desperate, having recently moved west from Manhattan – which, Trey gathered, he had *not* wanted to do – and he didn't know a soul in Chicago. Figuring the simplest way to go about things was to introduce the new arrival to Trey's own group of friends, it hadn't taken much ingenuity to engineer the crossing of their paths during lunch break.

Finding common ground was also not a problem. Generally, all guys who Trey hung around with liked cars, so when he'd struck up a conversation about the four-door Packard with the classy paint job he'd seen Alex come to school in the day before, that was it. Job done.

By the time classes were ready to begin again for the afternoon, Trey knew that Alex was, like him, an only child; that his father was some kind of businessman who ran a construction company; that Alex was a baseball fanatic, who naturally supported the New York Yankees (which was okay), and he could recite batting averages till the cows came home (which was less so). Best of all, though, was the fact that he was keen on photography. *Real* keen.

Taking a leaf out of Gramps's book – he was fond of saying that there was no time like the present – Trey caught up with Alex as they were leaving at the end of the school day and invited him to come over after classes on Friday. He could, Trey said, help him develop a film and make some prints, if he wanted.

Alex wanted.

They exchanged telephone numbers, agreed to get their respective parents' permission and were about to part company when the two-tone Packard four-door pulled up at the kerb and the uniformed chauffeur got out.

"You want a lift home?" Alex blurted out eagerly. "I live quite close to you...we could run you there."

Trey, who was normally dropped at school by his father, usually walked home, but this opportunity to maybe find out a few more details was too good a chance to miss. "Sure," he nodded. "Why not."

It was only a short journey, during which the only information Trey was able to glean was that the chauffeur's name was Davis. This was mainly because his attention was elsewhere, as he couldn't shake the feeling that they were being followed. But, what with the afternoon traffic being so heavy, he hadn't been able to spot anything out of the ordinary. And so by the time the chauffeur pulled up outside The Tavistock, Trey's apartment building, all there was left for him to do was say his goodbyes.

Trey scanned the street as he watched Alex's car drive away, but saw nothing worth commenting on. Saying hi to the doorman, he crossed the building's marbled foyer and got the elevator guy to take him up to the tenth floor.

That evening, as the maid came in to clear away the dinner plates, Trey asked if it would be all right to have a friend over the next day, after school.

"Who, dear?" his mother said, carefully placing her cutlery in the I-have-finished position on her plate.

"Alex. Alex Little."

"Is he a new friend?" asked Trey's father. "I don't recall you mentioning him before."

"He's just moved from New York, Pop. This is his first week at Mount Vernon."

"Well I've got a short trip to make, won't be back until late Saturday – Sophia?"

"I'll be out tomorrow night, but I'm sure that will be fine; although you *must* let Cook know that there will one extra, Trey." His mother dabbed the corners of her mouth with a white damask napkin. "You know how she *hates* surprises, dear."

"I'll do that, Mom."

"Well, son," Trey's father picked up his *Chicago Evening Post*, "I'm glad to see that you're abiding by the school motto."

"I am?"

"You must see it every day: *Societas cum fiducia* – fellowship with trust." His father opened the paper. "Would that more of our politicians lived by that credo."

"Oh…right…" Trey wasn't at all sure where politicians came into things, or that what he was doing fulfilled any part of the school motto, no matter which way you looked at it.

"What does this Alex Little's father do?"

"He has a construction company."

"No doubt called Little Skyscrapers Inc., eh, Sophie!" T. Drummond MacIntyre II raised both eyebrows and grinned broadly at his wife, who smiled sweetly back and rang the bell for the dessert to be served.

Joe Cullen came into the diner from parking up the Chrysler; the fastest way of getting to Chicago had ended up being to drive rather than waiting for a train. As days went, this had been a pretty decent one, apart from when he thought the kid had spotted him. He'd had to drop the auto way back in the traffic, and stay there the rest of the journey, just in case; it was somewhat easier following a mark who was a pedestrian, he had to say.

He walked over to the booth and sat down on the opposite side of the table from Dewey McGuigan. Dewey was nineteen and by no means the sharpest blade in the knife drawer, but – and it was a very big "but" – he was family. Kind of. He was Joe's wife's sister's son. And Joe had taken him on as a favour, as Dewey was, so his wife's sister said, "getting in with the wrong crowd" and needed someone to take him in hand. His not-so-bright father wasn't around to do the job himself as he was behind bars and only ten months into a five-year stretch for attempted bank robbery.

As Dewey was proof positive that the apple never fell very far from the tree, Joe had chosen to bring him along on this job, because to leave him alone and unsupervised in Topeka would've been an act of supreme foolishness on his part.

Joe picked up the menu. "What's the special tonight, Dewey?"

"Liver, Joe. With gravy, potatoes and peas."

"That so...? Think I'll have to go with the Salisbury steak, then."

"Right, good choice, Joe..." Dewey took out a cheap spiral-bound notepad and flicked through a couple of the lined pages. "You want all the notes and stuff I wrote down?"

"I'll look at them later, Dewey, but you did real good." Joe smiled encouragingly, glad that the kid hadn't figured out that he'd basically spent the day on a make-work task, designed to keep him out of his hair and out of trouble. "You ordered?"

Dewey shook his head. "Waited fer you, Joe. I'll have whatever you have."

"Good choice." Joe signalled the waitress, ordered two Salisbury steaks, all the trimmings, and two black coffees, then sat back and lit a cigarette. "How the other half live, eh, Dewey?"

"How d'you mean, Joe?"

"These kids, they get ferried here and there in fancy cars, with chauffeurs, no less; they live in fancy duplex apartments…" the waitress delivered the coffees and Joe reached for the sugar dispenser, "…they got cooks and maids, flunkies in the foyer and someone to press the elevator button for them. Nice life, right?" He poured a long stream of sugar into his mug and jangled the spoon around.

"Mr. Dunne, he has a pretty good life, too."

"Mr. Dunne worked hard for what *he's* got, Dewey." Joe stubbed out his cigarette. "Types like the MacIntyre kid, they get born with it all right there in their lap and don't appreciate what it is they been given – and, what's more likely, probably never will."

The waitress arrived carrying two plates of food in one hand and cutlery wrapped in paper napkins in the other. "Two Salls-berries, all the trimmings. You boys want sauce? We got the full choice: yellow, brown or red."

They ate in silence, Dewey taking Joe's lead in the matter. Only when they'd finished the apple pie à la mode Joe ordered, and were waiting for their third refill of coffee, did Dewey ask what they were going to do next. He'd been busting to find out as, frankly, he had no idea *how* they were going to get the film off a kid who lived ten floors up in a two-storey apartment with a uniformed doorman and all. It wasn't as if they could simply stroll into the place and take it.

"What we gonna do?" Joe offered Dewey a cigarette, which he declined. Of all the bad habits his mother worried about him picking up, smoking wasn't one of those he had. "Tomorrow we get that film and get us back to Topeka."

"We do? How?"

"Go right up there," Joe flicked a match alight with his thumb, "and take it."

Dewey was dumbstruck for a second or two. "We do?"

"Sure. We wait till the boy and his father leave, then, when the mother goes out, we go in."

"How do we know she's gonna go out?"

"Did she go out today, like I told you?" Dewey nodded. "Then we'll be fine."

"But what if she doesn't tomorrow, Joe?"

"She will. I made inquiries, she goes out *every* day."

"What about whoever else is up there?"

Joe leaned across the table. "Some maid's gonna stop us? I don't think so. Not with a gat stuck in her face, right?"

"Yeah, right." Dewey grinned: tomorrow looked like it was going to be some kind of day. "Sounds like a plan, Joe!"

"It do, don't it."

9 THE BEST-LAID PLANS

Joe's fisherman grandfather, so his own da had told him, was very fond of a phrase that went something like "If anything can go wrong at sea it generally does so, and sooner rather than later". And today that old and long-dead gentleman had been proved correct yet again. Notwithstanding that he and Dewey were on dry land and not on a boat.

Everything had looked like it was copacetic – the boy and his father had left the building, to the minute, the same time as they did the previous day, and then, a couple of hours later, a taxicab had pulled up and the mother had gone. Having impressed upon Dewey that he had nothing to do but look menacing, Joe checked that his piece was loaded – even though he didn't think he'd actually have any cause to use it – and they were ready to go.

Parking the car pretty close to the Tavistock building, should they need to exit at some speed, Joe straightened his hat and strolled up the sidewalk with Dewey at his heels. In his coat pocket there was a sealed heavyweight parchment envelope, the kind he knew lawyers used; it had the words "Mr. Curtis D. Marttensen" – the name of the person living below the MacIntyres' – typed on it, along with the words "PRIVATE & CONFIDENTIAL" underlined in red. In his wallet was a business card he'd made up the night before, using the little Kelsey printing kit he'd purchased, along with a cheap portable typewriter, from a stationery store. It claimed he was J.D. North and showed the details of a fake Detroit law office.

The story was that he had to deliver important legal documents to the said person, in person. Joe knew – because he'd gotten Marttensen's phone number from the book and called ahead – that the man was out of town, but he would insist that he, and his assistant, should deliver the letter to the apartment nonetheless.

They would then stop the lift at the eighth floor, as expected, and walk up the couple of flights to the MacIntyres' apartment on the tenth, and get to work.

The doorman had done *his* job to perfection, but then the tight-lipped, starch-collared type at the front desk heaved a real spanner in the works by refusing point-blank to let them take the letter up, and demanding it was left with him. Short of creating some sort of scene by slapping the guy's snoot or getting out his gun (which, as he aimed to do this job as quietly as possible, was not the way he wanted to play it) Joe had had little choice but to make an exit and come up with some kind of Plan B.

When the attempt to get into the building from round the back, where groceries and suchlike were delivered, also failed – neither of them looked remotely like delivery boys – Joe decided to retreat to the diner for a rethink and a late lunch of meatloaf, gravy and carrots. There was no way he could consider, deliberate and decide what to do next on an empty stomach.

The same as the day before, the two-tone Packard was waiting outside Mount Vernon when school let out, and although Trey would have preferred to walk, today was the day Alex was coming home with him, so he accepted a ride. Waiting on the back seat was Alex's camera, in its case.

Trey kept a weather eye out for signs of anyone following them, but saw nothing and got not one single tickle or twinge to suggest somebody was. A fact that was, he had to say, disappointing. As Mr. Little wasn't in the car, Davis, the chauffeur, let the boys get out by themselves at the Tavistock.

"Thought I'd bring this with me." Alex picked up his camera. "You know, just in case..."

"Sure," Trey grinned, "I know."

Alex slung the strap of the leatherette camera case over his shoulder. "You don't have to bother to come pick me up," he said to Davis as he got out. "It's only a couple of blocks. I'll walk home."

"You sure?" Davis queried.

"If I could do it in Manhattan, I can do it here, whatever my mom thinks. But don't tell her, right?"

"Not unless she asks." Davis shifted the car into gear. "I like this job."

Trey had only developed a film and made prints once before, so, while they ate the sandwiches and cookies that had been prepared for them, he and Alex pored over the "teach yourself" manual that had come with the darkroom equipment. When they were both sure they pretty much knew what they were doing, the two of them decamped upstairs to Trey's room and got to work organizing everything they were going to need.

"Okay..." Alex pushed his glasses up his nose and grinned, "...I think we're ready."

"Fine." Trey picked up his camera. "You figure out how much developer and fixer we're gonna need and I'll go in the darkroom, unload the film and put it in the tank..."

Half an hour later a strip of negative film with twenty-four pictures on it was drying off in the darkroom – a record of the events Trey had thought worth recording during the last week or so of his stay on the Circle M. (He'd had the rest of his films developed and printed down in Topeka.)

As soon as the film was dry they set to work making the prints. They stood side by side staring at a liquid-filled tray, Alex rocking it slightly, as they waited for the first couple of prints to develop in front of their eyes. It all began very, very slowly, but then, in the deep red light, they could make out the images beginning to appear one after the other on the blank sheets of paper.

"Kind of like magic, right?" Trey said, watching as the last picture he'd taken at the T-Bone ranch birthday party – the one of the man called Tony Burrell posing with the Duesenberg – came into view. "I mean, I know it's all chemicals and such, but still..."

"That looks like Uncle Mario's car!"

Trey's hand stopped in mid-air as he dropped the print into a rinse bath. "That's your *uncle's* car?"

"Yeah, you know, the pretend kind of uncle who's your dad's friend?"

Trey put the black-and-white print in the stop bath, hardly able to believe what he was hearing. How many people called Mario could there be who owned a two-seater Duesenberg boat-tail coupé? "Is your uncle's car blue, with red leather seats?"

"Yeah, it is...why?"

"Just wondered..." Trey said, all the time thinking, If "Uncle" Mario is as much of a wise guy as he looks, then Alex Little's father certainly knows some people. He rinsed the print again and put it in the fixer bath. "Is he in the construction business, too, your Uncle Mario?"

"No, he's in haulage, my dad says...look, it *is* Uncle Mario!" Alex peered at the second print, pointing at the woman in the picture. "Wonder who that is with him?"

"Think I heard him say it was his secretary..."

"Jeepers!" Alex looked at his watch, examining it in the red light. "That the time? I'd better get my skates on or my mom'll start wondering where I am and have the St Bernards out looking for me. Again..."

Dewey McGuigan was so bored his brain hurt; not to mention he'd run out of chewing gum. Joe had got him watching the darn apartment building, again, while he did something else. Joe hadn't cared to mention what that something involved, but Dewey was certain that it had to be entirely more interesting than what *he'd* been up to.

He checked his watch. It was not the *most* reliable timepiece (in that it lost about an hour a day, except it did so as regular as, well, clockwork) but, that being said, it showed he'd been hanging round for three some hours, since before the two boys had been dropped off – in a chauffeur-driven car, exactly like Joe had told him. He was going to need his shoes resoled if he did much more pavement-pounding (Joe had also told him to keep on the move, so he didn't look suspicious; and to keep the front entrance of the building in sight at the same time – which was no mean feat, he had to say).

And then everything started to happen at once. He saw a boy come out of the Tavistock in a uniform he recognized. At first Dewey was confused – he couldn't tell from behind which one of the two boys it was – then he spotted the camera case slung over his shoulder, and he figured this was when he should use his gumption. So he began following the boy.

Dewey was in the middle of trying to figure out whether he should carry on tailing the kid, or whether he should simply run up and grab the camera, when he saw Joe driving down the street in the Chrysler, and he had an idea. He waved excitedly, pointing at the boy and then at the car. Joe waved back out of the open window, giving him the thumbs up, and slowed down as he steered towards the sidewalk.

Speeding up, Dewey got to the boy at pretty much the same time as Joe brought the Chrysler to a halt. Grabbing the kid, Dewey wrenched open the rear door and flung the boy in, then leaped in himself and slammed the door shut.

"I got it, Joe!" he shouted. "I got the camera!"

10 POINT OF VIEW

Trey always kept a pair of binoculars on the window ledge in the lounge – this high up the world looked surprisingly different, and he was astonished at how much time he could waste confirming that fact. Today, though, he was waiting to locate Alex walking off home. He was also trying to make sense of the evidence he'd discovered upstairs in the darkroom: not only had he seen Alex's dad (who, it had to be said, did not look one bit like a hoodlum) with Bad Frank and the Tall Suit (who very much did), he *also* turned out to be pals with a similar-looking type of guy called Mario. *Uncle* Mario, no less.

Then Trey saw Alex, ten floors below, striding up the street. He adjusted the focus, wondering if Alex would look up and wave; they had, he had to admit, become fast friends over the afternoon. Trey was just thinking that, while there was no doubt that Alex was a swot, he was a swot with one terrific sense of humour, when he saw someone appear out of nowhere and rush up behind his new pal. Trey's jaw dropped like a flag with no wind as he stood and watched Alex being thrown into the back of a brown saloon car that had pulled up at the kerb.

For a second Trey froze, the binoculars glued to his face. Had he just seen a kidnapping, in broad daylight?

The car began to move and Trey leaned forward, banging his binoculars on the window. Madly grabbing for the fastener, he pulled the window open and leaned out to see the car almost cause an accident as it made a screeching right onto the cross street and accelerated away. Leaning even further out, the tips of his toe-capped shoes *barely* touching the parquet floor, Trey just managed to focus on the blue licence plate of the car, which looked like a fairly recent Chrysler.

Muttering "27–636...27–636...27–636..." to himself, Trey hauled himself back in and ran over to his mother's writing desk, grabbed a pencil and scribbled the numbers down on the pad she always kept there, by the phone. Then he stood quite still, breathing hard, the binoculars gripped in his left hand, the pencil in his right. What on earth was he going to do now?

"What in tarnation are you *doing*, Dewey?" Joe peered over into the rear of the car to see a tangle of arms and legs. "And who the *heck* is that?"

"Step on the gas, Joe, we gotta get outta here – *ow!*" Dewey winced as an elbow jabbed him in the face.

"*YOU* LET *ME* OUT OF HERE – YOU, YOU...!"

"Dang it, Dewey, what the *heck* you done now?"

"It's the kid with the camera, Joe, from the building!"

"You can't just..." The sound of crunching gears was followed by some of what Dewey's mom would've called "colourful language" and the shriek of tyres as Joe sped away from what he was well aware was now the scene of a crime: abduction. He made a hasty and almost catastrophic right turn at the first junction he came to.

A few minutes later (some of the longest minutes in history, from Dewey's point of view, as he spent them wrestling with this kid who seemed to have turned into a crazed mutt, and certainly had a mouth on him) Joe skidded to a halt in a dingy and deserted back alley, yanked up the hand brake and exited the car.

"Dewey," Joe opened the rear door, "you get out the car with that kid *NOW!*"

"Okay, but he'll lamp me again if—"

"Don't 'but' me, sunshine." Joe grabbed a hold of Dewey's arm and pulled. "Let go of the kid, Dewey."

Hastily untangling himself, Dewey scuttled out into the alley, pulling down his crumpled jacket and smoothing back his mussed-up hair. "Sheesh, Joe, didya see what he did to me?"

"Who is he, Dewey?" Joe peered into the car. "Who the heck are you, kid?"

"You grab me off of the street, mister, and you don't even know who I *am*?"

"I toldya, Joe, I saw him coming out the building and he had the camera, and then I saw you and I thought..."

"You thought what?" Joe turned to look despairingly at his wife's sister's boy. "I never asked you to think... This ain't the MacIntyre boy, you got *the wrong kid*! So that would make it *a* camera, and not *the* camera. And anyway, it's the dadblamed *film* we're after, you numskull..."

"Who *are* you guys?" said a voice from inside the car. "Dingus and Duckweed?"

"Watch it, kid." Joe pushed Dewey behind him and jerked a thumb down the alley. "There's been a mistake, so you get yourself out the car and on your way and let that be the end of it, 'kay?"

"The end of it?" Alex sat up and straightened his glasses. "You guys just kidnapped me!"

"And now we're *un*-kidnapping you. We've had second thoughts. Go..." Joe made impatient get-outta-here motions with his hand.

Alex got up off the floor, clutched the camera to him and stepped out of the car, backing away from Joe and Dewey. "You can't *un*-kidnap someone."

"We just did, kid, now scram before I change my mind!" Joe reached into his jacket and took out his pistol. "Git!"

Not needing to be told again, Alex continued backing down the alley towards the street. "You won't get away with this!" he yelled as he got there.

"Amscray, idkay," Joe muttered, tucking his pistol back into his shoulder holster, "and good riddance." Turning round he landed a couple of swift flat-handed slaps on Dewey, much to the boy's surprise, and got back in the driving seat.

"Wha...?" Dewey rubbed his stinging cheeks. "Heck, Joe!"

"Get in the car. Get in the darn car before I run you over..."

Trey stood staring at the phone. One voice in his head was yelling at him to pick up the handset and call the cops, which seemed like an entirely logical thing to do when you'd just seen someone grabbed and thrown in the back of a car. But he couldn't ignore the *other* voice. The one that was telling him to hold on a minute, and remember who this person who'd been hijacked happened to be: he was, after all, the son of a man who had undoubted mob connections.

Question: would the police know about those connections, too? And if they did, because of who his father knew, would they even *care* if Alex had been kidnapped? Answer: who knew? But in a *Black Ace* story he'd read recently, a guy who worked for a mobster, and didn't *know* he was a mobster, got blamed for stuff he didn't do. It was called *Guilty by Association* and hadn't had a happy ending. Then a worse thought occurred to him: what if Alex's dad was a *real* mobster? Which set Trey to wondering if the cops actually had to bother when bad guys did things to *other* bad guys.

And then again, were the police going to believe a word he said when he told them what he'd seen? Because he had no proof; he'd been looking through a pair of binoculars, and not the viewfinder of a camera, at the time. And he was only a kid.

What he needed was some grown-up type to do the talking for him. But his mother was out and even if his pop had been around, and not off on another of his business trips, Trey didn't think he could convince him that they should go to the cops. Gramps, maybe, but he was still down in Topeka on the ranch. Except, come to think of it, Gramps had completely ignored what Trey had told him about meeting Tall Suit and Bad Frank – and the man he now knew was Alex's dad – on the road to the T-Bone ranch.

And then it dawned on him what he *really* needed!

A detective. A sleuth, a PI, a gumshoe, a whatever-the-heck-you-wanted-to-call-them: someone who knew about hoodlums and the way they worked, and also knew how to deal with the police, because they were used to being stuck in a small room, with a light shining in their face, being grilled for hour upon hour. He needed someone like Trent Gripp.

But where did you find a *real* detective at – Trey looked at his watch – a quarter to six on a Friday afternoon? He snapped his fingers and ran down the hall like he had the Devil himself biting at his heels. His only chance, and he realized it was a slim one, was going to be found in the yellow pages business directory he knew his pop kept on a shelf in his study. Somewhere in Chicago there had to be somebody who could help him...

11 THE REAL WORLD

It was now five minutes to six and Trey was beginning to realize that in the real world, as opposed to what occurred in the novelettes he read, things were different; come six o'clock on a Friday evening, it seemed even private investigators might well be hanging up their hats and looking forward to a weekend off. He had been connected to seven numbers so far and only two had had someone in the office to pick up the phone – worse, both of the people who'd answered had accused him of making a prank call and one had tersely reminded him that it wasn't Hallowe'en for another month or so, bud.

Trey looked at the next number in the directory under the heading "Detective Agencies" and saw that it was for an outfit that went by the name of Pisbo Investigations, Inc. He dialled the number, nervously drumming his fingers on his pop's desktop as he wondered exactly how many numbers he should call before he gave up and set about thinking of something...

"Hello?"

A bright, cheery female voice at the other end of the line interrupted Trey's musings.

"Pisbo Investigations, discretion is the first word in our dictionary!"

It is? thought Trey, at a loss for words.

"Excuse me? Anyone there?"

"Hi, yes..."

"And what can we do for you?"

"I, um...I think my friend has been kidnapped..." Trey blurted out, then waited to be told he should stop wasting people's time. But the rebuff never came.

"Kidnapped, why that's *terrible*! You want us to help you get them back?"

"Well, yeah, sure..."

"Has a ransom demand been made, and have you been told not to contact the police, which is why you're contacting us, sir?"

Sir? Trey liked the sound of that and was about to answer when he heard a man's voice in the background call out the name "Velma". Then Velma, if that was who he was talking to, must've put her hand over the receiver as he couldn't make out what she said back. He was about to say something when Velma spoke first.

"I think you should come down to the office *right away*! What did you say your name was, sir?"

"I didn't yet, but it's T. Drummond MacIntyre. The third."

"The third?"

"Yeah..."

"The third, okay..."

Trey thought he could hear the scratch of pencil on paper as a note was being made, and was relieved he'd at last found *some*one who took him and his situation seriously.

"What's the 'T' stand for?"

"The 'T'? Oh..." Trey was not over-fond of his given name, and tried to ignore its existence, but seeing as how this was official business he figured he should answer the question. "It's Theodore, but people call me Trey."

"Keen!"

Trey held the handset away and looked at it, perplexed, then put it back to his ear. "Look..."

"Are you gonna come to the office, or not?" the girl said. "Mr. Pisbo won't be here all night."

"Well..."

"Y'do want to get your friend back, dontcha?"

"Sure I do...so when will Mr. Pisbo be there till?" Trey looked at his watch and saw that it was now five past six, over forty minutes since Alex had been thrown in the back of some car.

"Oh I should say at *least* another hour or so."

Trey glanced at the address given in the directory, which was downtown. He could make it, if he put his skates on. "I'll be there!" he said and slammed the phone down.

It was now almost seven o'clock and the sun was setting as Trey stood on the sidewalk outside the building: five storeys of offices in the middle of a city block which had definitely seen better days. Considering what he'd had to do to finesse his way out of the apartment and find his way downtown, it was amazing he was there at all.

As his father had been called away on business, and would not be back until Saturday night, and his mother was out and not expected home until late, Cook (whose surname, weirdly enough, was Cooke) was in charge. It was a job she took excessively seriously, in Trey's opinion. Eventually, after what he considered to have been one of his best performances, she had swallowed the story about him having been invited to dinner at his new friend's house pretty much hook, line and sinker.

Trey then gathered together all the mazuma he could get his hands on, the total coming to $76 and 39 cents; he took all the notes and put them in an envelope. He hadn't asked what Mr. Pisbo's rates were (and the advertisement didn't say) and all he could hope was that he had enough cash not to be shown the door immediately. Trent Gripp charged twenty-five dollars a day, plus expenses, but what an *actual* PI would cost Trey had no idea. Chucking his notebook and the prints he and Alex had made into his satchel, and nearly forgetting the scrap of notepaper with the registration number on it, he'd exited the apartment building as if on wheels. Which, standing on the sidewalk, watching the early evening traffic zip by, he'd wished he had; instead, he'd had to run to the nearest train station and take the elevated downtown.

The address he'd made a note of said that he could find Pisbo Investigations, Inc. in Suite 419b, and, sure enough, the directory on the wall of the drab foyer confirmed that a company of that name was on the fourth floor. Trey called the elevator, but it took so long (and sounded, as Gramps would no doubt have said, like it'd originally been installed in the Ark as it came down) that in the end he figured it'd be quicker, and possibly safer, to walk.

And then there he was, slightly out of breath, standing in front of a brown door, with *Pisbo Investigations, Inc.* painted on it in faded gold letters, wondering what the heck he thought he was doing. He was just about to turn around and go right back to the Tavistock, because this was, he realized, a *very* stupid idea, when the door opened.

12 2 + 2 = 5

The moment he'd gotten out of the alley and was making a dash for home, Alex knew one thing: he was not going to tell *anyone* at home, least of all his mom, what had just occurred. If his father found out there'd been a kidnap attempt it would be bad enough, but his mom...it hardly bore thinking about. She would blow a whole fusebox full of fuses and he would be under armed guard even when he went to the john – at home!

His life would not be worth living.

He'd run a couple of hundred yards when he stopped, found a pencil stub and a scrap of paper in one of his pockets and scribbled down the registration plate of the car, as best as he could remember it; he'd sworn those two weren't going to get away with what they'd done, and he'd meant it! Then, using a shop window, Alex had quickly brushed himself down as best he could, straightened his tie and combed his hair back. Once he was pretty sure he'd pass a cursory inspection he set off again, deciding as he went that he'd steer well clear of the front door and use the tradesmen's entrance instead; that way he was much less likely to run into his mom until he'd made completely sure there were no telltale signs of the fracas for her to pick up on. Because he *had* to keep this all to himself.

Except…

He'd come to a halt again, a couple of people behind him on the sidewalk nearly bumping into him. What about Trey? From what he'd gathered from the conversation between the two guys involved (Joe, the older one, and the sap, called Dewey) the person they were *really* after was Trey. What was it the one called Joe had said? "*It ain't the MacIntyre boy!*" – the words were still ringing in his ears. So, the person they'd wanted *had* to be Trey.

Alex had hotfooted it the rest of the way home.

Alex sat on his bed and, for the first time since he'd been bodily picked up off the street outside Trey's apartment building and hurled into some car, allowed himself to relax. As the tension slowly drained out of him, like used engine oil from a sump, he began to shake and had to bite his lower lip, grab the white candlewick bedspread and make himself sit up straight: he wasn't going to snivel...he was not!

Now he stood up. He couldn't sit around, he *must* warn Trey that there were a couple of no-goods on the lookout for him and his camera! As he raced out of his room and made for the stairs he realized that, in actual fact, the guy called Joe had *actually* said it was some film they were after. Taking the stairs two and three at a time he thundered into the hallway, skidded sideways across the carpet and ran to the alcove where the phone stood, like a holy object, on an inlaid walnut table.

"Alex?" His mother's voice came from the front lounge; for all that she was tiny, she could make a noise like a Hudson River foghorn when she wanted to be heard.

"Yes, Mom?"

"What have I told you about running in the house, sweety-pie?"

"Yes, Mom..."

"Don't."

"Yes – I mean no, Mom…" Alex picked up the receiver as quietly as he could, and got the piece of paper with Trey's home number on it out of his pocket as he waited for the operator.

"Could you close the door, sweety-pie? I'm sure there's a draught…we *have* to live on the windiest block in this city, you know."

Alex put the phone down, did as he'd been asked, and, when he picked it up again, found someone asking if there was anyone there. After giving the lady at the local switchboard Trey's number, and while he waited to be put through, he checked his wristwatch. It was twenty to six.

"MacIntyre residence, how may I help you?"

"Can I speak to Trey, please?" Alex thought the person at the other end of the line sounded like the maid who'd let them into the house earlier in the day.

"I'm sorry, but young Mr. MacIntyre is not here at present."

"Not there?" Alex frowned. "Where is he?"

"I'm sorry, I don't know that."

"Okay, okay…when's he coming back?"

"I'm sorry…"

"You don't know that either?" Alex shook his head. "Right, look, when he *does* come back, could you tell him to call Alex Little. It's *very* important."

"I will."

"Thank you." Alex heard the phone being put down and, slowly lowering his own receiver, he wondered what on earth he was going to do now.

"Who were you talking to, dear?"

Alex looked up to find his mom had come out into the hallway. "Me? Oh...yeah...um, I was talking to..." Alex's brain finally slipped into gear "...I was talking to the MacIntyres, y'know, just saying thanks for having me."

"Very thoughtful, dear." His mom smiled at him. "Now could you go and put anything you think you're going to need in a valise, we're leaving in about half an hour."

"Leaving? For where?"

"The country, somewhere...friends of your father's. Didn't I tell you? We're going for the weekend..."

13 A FILE IS OPENED

"You must be T. Drummond MacIntyre. The third."

The girl who was standing in the doorway was maybe an inch or so shorter than him, kind of his age, with a round, quite pretty face and brown hair cut in a bob with the straightest fringe Trey had ever seen. And her eyes were a soft yellowy green, like moss...

"Or are you maybe some kid wandered in off the street and just *happened* to find themselves outside Suite 419b?"

"No..."

"Good, now come in quick before he hears you!" The girl grabbed Trey's arm and pulled him into the outer office, quietly shutting the door. They stood facing each other in a small linoleum-floored room with a worn, two-seater settee, a grey, three-drawer filing cabinet, a hat-stand, a desk and a wooden swivel chair.

"He?" queried Trey.

"My father." The girl's moss-green eyes flicked to the right.

"Your father?"

"You won't get far in this world just constantly repeating everything anyone says to you, y'know."

"I do not...who are you, anyway?" Trey looked round for the person he'd talked to on the phone, and then it clicked. "*You're* Velma?"

To his left, out of the corner of his eye, Trey saw a door open and a man appear.

"Velma?" The man, not too tall – a kind of normal-looking guy in a suit, waistcoat and tie, with thinning hair combed back – frowned as he came into the outer office; he did not look like Trey's idea of a Private Eye. "I told you before about inviting friends up here to the office."

"He isn't a friend, Mr. Pisbo."

"Velma, will you *please* stop calling me Mr. Pisbo? You do not work for me."

"I do so – you pay me for what I do when I'm here, which is a *lot*!"

Trey saw the man he assumed must be the owner of the business – and, if he wasn't much mistaken, the girl's father – sigh deeply as he raised his eyebrows. Right at that moment Trey knew exactly how the man felt: exasperated! This dumb Dora had led him *all* the way downtown on what could turn out to be a wild goose chase – wasting not only his valuable time but also his train fare – if her father refused to listen to what he had to say.

"And he's not a friend." Velma made a "so *there*" face. "He's a *client*."

"Client? What client, Velma? What have you been up to?"

"Just answering your phone. While you were, you know, *otherwise engaged*."

"Son," Mr. Pisbo, turned towards Trey, "why are you here?"

"*His* friend's been kidnapped." Velma went and sat behind the desk, picked up a black ring binder and pointed at it. "I wrote it in the call log – which *you* never use like you should do – at five after six. His name's T. Drummond MacIntyre III, the 'T' stands for Theodore, but his friends call him Trey. So, you going to invite him into your office and ask him some questions, Mr..."

Mr. Pisbo looked daggers at his daughter. "Okay, okay... *Dad*."

"Right." Mr. Pisbo distractedly rubbed his not particularly square jaw, which showed a dark, well-defined five o'clock shadow. "You," he pointed at Trey, "you come with me and tell me what the *heck* this is all about, and you," he pointed at his daughter, "you said you were talking to a friend when I got back from the washroom. So stay where you are – and leave the phone alone."

Velma got up, pencil and yellow legal pad in hand. "Who's gonna take notes? Y'gotta have *notes*!"

"Jeez..." Mr. Pisbo made a face that said more than words ever could, and went back into his office.

"Well, go on." Velma came round the desk. "We got a case to solve!"

Trey sat in the chair opposite Mr. Pisbo (Frederick K. Pisbo, according to the nameplate on the door to his office). He'd explained everything, right from when he'd come across the Buick Monarch with the flat tyre that late August morning. Mr. Pisbo had asked one or two questions, but mainly let Trey talk while Velma took notes. On the desk was the piece of paper with the note of the kidnappers' registration number and the two black-and-white pictures he'd developed and printed with Alex. When Trey had finished, Mr. Pisbo picked up one of the prints and looked at it very closely.

"Who'd you say this was?" He held up the picture of the man posing by the Duesenberg.

Trey referred to his own notebook. "Tony Burrell." He looked across at Velma. "That's with a double 'r' and double 'l'."

"Much appreciated…" Velma rubbed something out with the eraser on the end of her pencil.

"And this guy?" Mr. Pisbo indicated the second photo.

"Mario. Alex said his name was Mario, but I didn't get a surname, sorry."

"Not to worry. Now this Alex…" Mr. Pisbo cast about for something on his fairly untidy desk.

"Little," said Velma without looking up. "Trey said his name's Alex Little."

"Right, I knew that. Now this Alex Little – you say you saw his father, who is from New York and something in construction, with a tall guy in a suit, and some goon called Frank, and they were all going to the T-Bone ranch, which is owned by someone your grandfather has a beef with called Bowyer Dunne. Correct?"

Trey nodded.

"Okeedoke…" Mr. Pisbo sat back in his chair and took a cigarette out of a pack of Camels, but didn't light it; his daughter (whom he usually had every other weekend – except for now, what with her mother having gone to Saginaw for two weeks to stay with her *equally* noxious sister) did not approve. "There *anything* else you can tell me about this, kid? Anything at all?"

"I've told you the lot, Mr. Pisbo, honest!"

"What about the registration?" Mr. Pisbo picked up the piece of paper. "You remember if you saw the state, or a year?"

"No..." Trey screwed up his face in concentration. "Can't remember if I saw that, just wrote the number down."

"What colour was the plate?" Fred Pisbo tamped the cigarette on his desk, but still didn't pick up the book of matches by his left hand.

Trey's face brightened. "It was blue, Mr. Pisbo, blue with white lettering!"

Velma got up and went to the bookshelf and after a couple of seconds picked up a slim soft-cover booklet.

Mr. Pisbo put the unlit cigarette down. "How'd you know where that was?"

"Who reorganized your reference books so you'd know what was where?" Velma flicked through the pages, then stopped. "White on a blue background... looks to me like that's most probably Kansas on a 1926 plate, Dad."

"Really?" Mr. Pisbo's face took on a distinct "well-I-never" look.

"So d'you believe me now, about the kidnapping? You do, right? And you'll help?" Trey pulled the envelope with his money in it out of his jacket pocket and put it on the desk. "I can pay…"

"Hold on a minute, whoa!" Mr. Pisbo leaned *way* back in his chair, eyebrows raised. "First off, are you positive your friend has been kidnapped? Did you call him to check you didn't just see it all wrong and he's at home right now with a glass of chocolate milk?"

"No…I didn't have time yet; I had to get here before you left."

Mr. Pisbo pushed the phone towards Trey. "Try now."

Trey looked at Velma, who shrugged. *Could* he have got this whole thing completely upside down? He picked up the receiver, that being the only way he was going to find out, gave the operator Alex's number out of his notebook and waited.

Two minutes later he put the phone down. "He's not there. The maid said no one was there, that they'd all gone to the country for the weekend."

"Maybe they have." Mr. Pisbo moved the phone back to where it usually sat on his desk.

"The cops probably told them that was what to say,"

said Velma, nodding sagely, "you know, so the kidnapping was all kept secret and out of the news? They say, once the story gets in the papers, *you* are in the morgue. If you're the victim..."

Lost in thought for the moment, Mr. Pisbo ignored his daughter's opining. These were, he had to admit, interesting times in Chicago, especially in his line of business. These days a private investigator had to be *extremely* careful what he did, and who he did it for, as it had never been easier to tread on the wrong toes. If you didn't know who the movers and the shakers were, on both sides of the law in this man's town, then you could end up in *real* trouble. And Fred K. Pisbo had enough trouble on his plate dealing with an ex-wife – Velma's harpy of a mother – to want any more, if it could be helped.

The thing of it was, while his daughter might well be entirely correct that he was a tad disorganized, Fred was a man who made it his business to know things. And he was pretty sure that Alex's father, whose business card no doubt purported that he was Mr. Nathan Little, was in actual fact Nate "The Book" Klein. He'd heard rumours about Nate Klein; that the American Building Corp., his successful construction business, was also a front for the Mob, used to launder millions of dollars in illegally generated funds. On the other hand, why he'd relocated from New York to Chicago he had no idea.

But what Fred *did* know was that kidnapping the man's son was a bad thing to do, if you were planning on a long and happy retirement. Whereas, getting the boy back in one piece could do wonders for your reputation, not to say bank balance.

"Okay, son…" Fred Pisbo sat forward, smiling broadly, and stuck out his right hand. "I'm on board!"

14 ALL DOWN TO THE TIMING

Trey sat opposite Velma at a table-for-two towards the back of a diner called diMaggio's; a popular place this Friday night. There was, disconcertingly, a small, but perky red rose in a cheap glass vase between them.

This was not quite how he'd seen his evening playing out, but once he'd let slip that he was going to have to make up some story for Mrs. Cooke about why he was home early from the dinner he was supposed to be at, Velma had insisted he ate with them. Her father had agreed and put on quite a snappy hat, taking them down to the restaurant where he then said he had some work to do and he'd be back. Leaving Trey alone with a girl. One he hardly knew, and, on top of that, someone he was not at all sure what he thought about.

It was Velma who broke the awkward silence.

"They do great spaghetti and meatballs here. Also, the *osso bucco* is delicious, if you like veal that is, but then it should be as these guys who run this place are all from Milan. I think *I* might have the Kansas City strip steak, though, seeing as it's Friday night and Mr. Pisbo's paying."

"D'you do that often?"

"Do what?" Velma frowned as she watched the busboy put two glasses of water on the table, along with some breadsticks.

"Pretend to work up there," Trey jerked his head back, "in the office."

"Pre*tend*?" Velma's mouth made a small, annoyed "o". "I like that! I get a dollar a day when I'm there, and I earn it, buster...I put in the hours, let me tell you."

"But you got me down here under false pretences! Your dad might've not taken the case, and *then* where would I have been? Nowhere, is where!"

"But he did, didn't he. Right?"

As Velma was, in fact, one hundred per cent right, Trey knew there was little point in trying to push the argument any further. And although an apology for leading him up the garden path would be nice, he realized one was highly unlikely. Velma, he could see, was not so big on being sorry.

"You think he can figure this out, your dad?"

"Sure." Velma snapped a breadstick in two and offered half to Trey, who took it. "He's good."

"He is?"

"Why d'you sound so surprised?" Velma's lips pursed, two sharp frown lines appearing between her eyebrows.

"I didn't! I meant 'I'm *sure* he is'."

"Just seeing as I help out doesn't mean he can't afford a secretary...he just had to let the last one go as she was about as useful as a sieve if you were thirsty. She was blonde, out of a bottle, which also didn't help. I think my dad only employed her to give my mother the heebies. Which it did, I can tell you. I told him to make sure the next one has a face could break mirrors, *if* he wants an easier life. Which you'd think he would, considering."

Trey watched Velma as she talked and flicked through the menu. He had never met *anyone* capable of carrying on, at length, like she could; truth to tell, he didn't spend much time with girls his own age, partly out of choice and partly because Mount Vernon

Academy was an all-boy institution. Which made Velma something of a curiosity. Picking up his menu, Trey wondered what it was like having parents who got on so bad they ended up hating each other and getting divorced.

Trey and Velma were about done, having finished off the excellent ice cream sodas they'd chosen for dessert, when Fred Pisbo came back into the diner, pushed another table up next to theirs and sat down.

"Well, looks like you two have been at the trough," he said, pushing his hat back and looking over his shoulder. "What's good tonight, Gino?"

"*Tutto, come sempre!*" The elderly man working behind the bar waved his arms in a flamboyant, all-encompassing gesture.

"How can I choose when everything's good, Gino?"

Velma raised her eyebrows. "They do this *every* time...he'll have the lasagne, Gino, like he always does! So, Dad, what didya find out?"

"Oh, this, that and the other...but I got someone coming by later who can maybe help me out some more."

"Who?"

"You ever meet Shady? Shady Jones?" Velma shook

her head. "No? Okay, thought he might've been up to the office when you were around."

"Who is he?" asked Trey.

"He's like the invisible man…as in he's not a very *noticeable* kind of guy, not someone you remember so much. But he listens, got ears like a bat – not as big, mind you, but he's a genius at hearing stuff. And, as he's also a terrific waiter, he gets around some high-table places, not to mention low dives, all over town."

"Why's he called Shady, he crooked as well, Dad?"

"Nah. Given name's Shadrach. Got two brothers naturally called Meshach and Abednego; they go by Shack and Abbey, Shady tells me."

As Mr. Pisbo explained to Velma that Shady Jones was from the South – somewhere in Alabama, he thought – then went on to enquire about her schoolwork, Trey's attention wandered and he noticed two men come into the diner. One was short, the other tall, like Laurel and Hardy, except the big guy wasn't fat and didn't have a mustache. Gino behind the bar appeared extremely flustered by their arrival, acting like Trey had seen certain people act around his pop when he'd been with him on factory visits. All "Yes, Mr. MacIntyre! No, Mr. MacIntyre! *Anything* you say, Mr. MacIntyre!", which was not like Gino had been with any other customers all evening.

Trey watched as Gino shepherded the two men towards the rear of the restaurant, an episode missed by Mr. Pisbo, who was deep in conversation with his daughter. After a moment's consideration Trey pushed his chair back. "Excuse me, but I have to go to the washroom."

"Down the back." Mr. Pisbo nodded the way Gino had walked. "They claim it's so clean you could eat off the floor, but I would not recommend such a course of action myself... Now, Velma, about your last Math report card..."

Trey left Velma to explain herself and set off. He actually could do with going to the toilet, but the real thing of it was his gut: he felt *sure* something was up with those two guys and the old man Gino. And in the last chapter he'd read of *How to Become a Private Eye in 10 Easy Lessons*, Austin J. Randall had been at pains to point out that a good PI had to develop his instincts and be prepared to rely on them, if he was going to have any chance of getting on in the business. Walking down the narrow, low-lit passage he made a mental note to ask Mr. Pisbo if he'd heard of Austin J. Randall. He might've, it being, as his gramps was fond of saying, a very small world.

A couple of yards down, the passage turned a corner to the right and he saw a door. A sign on it said *Toilette*, underneath which was written *Uomini e Donne*. Ignoring it he carried on towards the sound of voices, which were coming from where the corridor took a sharp left. He could hear one person talking fast in a slightly whiney, high-pitched voice; it had to be Gino. Then there was another voice, slower and more emphatic. Gino was not happy, that much was obvious. Trey took a few more very careful steps, then stopped, glancing behind him to check that no one was there, and listened.

"But Mr. Cavallo..."

"Look at it this way, old man – it's like ten dollars a week, and we don't make you pay for Sunday; so you can go to church, light a few candles and give thanks that you're being looked after so well. Everyone needs insurance, right?"

Trey mouthed a silent, triumphal *"YES!"* to celebrate being right about what was going on, then immediately felt bad, as what was happening would not come under the heading of good news in anybody's book. Gino was, after all, being shaken down by gangsters.

"I already *got* insurance, Mr. Cavallo!"

"Not like ours, Gino. Ours is *very* effective...the other type, something happens, they pay; this way, you pay and *nothing* happens. Nothing. Guaranteed. On the other hand, I see a lot of wood around, and no doubt olive oil, grappa and suchlike...what was that phrase

I heard the other day, Ricco? That was it: 'a highly combustible combination'."

"But Mr. Cavallo..."

"You think about it, Gino. Overnight. Ricco'll be back tomorrow."

Trey, who'd been concentrating on listening to the conversation, and keeping an ear out for anyone else in search of the washroom, heard the scrape of leather soles on floorboards and realized, too late, that he should make a move, and pronto. Caught like a cockroach in the middle of the kitchen floor when the light was turned on, Trey found himself looking for somewhere dark to hide, while in front of him appeared the smaller of the two men who'd come into the diner – Mr. Cavallo he presumed. Behind him came the bigger one, Ricco. He couldn't see Gino.

"Who're you, kid?" Mr. Cavallo snapped his fingers. "Gino, who's this kid?"

Gino's head came into view in the gap between Ricco and the wall. "A customer. He's a customer."

"What you doing here, customer? What?"

"I, um...the washroom?" Trey looked left and right, shrugging, with his palms up.

"You must be stupid, or something." Mr. Cavallo jerked a stumpy thumb at the door with the really quite large *Toilette* sign on it. "As you don't sound to me

120

like you just got off no boat."

"Me? No, but I, um..." Trey felt as if his brain was spinning like a tyre on an icy road as he tried to think of some sort of legit excuse for what he was doing there, "...I have, you know, a real bad case of myopia."

"You have a *what*?" Mr. Cavallo jerked back, like he'd been pushed, a shocked expression on his jowly face. "Is that catching? I'm sure I heard that was catching – Gino, you let people with *diseases* in here? There should be a law against doing that!"

"I'm short-sighted..." Trey screwed his eyes up in an exaggerated squint, just to make sure the message got through. "I left my glasses behind."

"Why'n't you say so inna first place..." Mr. Cavallo patted his chest and took a deep breath. "I can feel my heart thumping nineteen to the dozen, all over the damn place."

"Everything all right?" Mr. Pisbo came right up behind Trey and put a hand on his shoulder. "Wondered where you could've gotten to."

"This your boy?" Mr. Cavallo eyeballed Trey like he was something that'd just crawled out of a drain – one which, personally, *he* wouldn't touch with a long pole.

"With me, not *of* me."

"Whatever...kids that're half-blind with some condition shouldn't be let to wander around."

Mr. Cavallo, followed by a frowning Ricco, moved swiftly past them, hurrying down the passage and round the corner, leaving Trey and Mr. Pisbo looking at Gino.

"Friends of yours, Gino?"

Gino stood up a bit straighter and smoothed down his white apron; he looked at Mr. Pisbo, a "what-can-we-do?" expression on his lined face, and said nothing.

"I can help, just ask, right?"

Gino nodded. "Sure."

Mr. Pisbo ushered Trey in front and scooted him back towards the restaurant, leaving Gino alone with his thoughts. "What the *heck* were you up to back there, young man?" He leaned forward and hissed in Trey's ear. *"Do you know who that was?"*

"I..."

"For your information, that was Lucca Cavallo, and you do not *ever* go sneaking up on Lucca Cavallo. Or anyone else from his side of the street, come to that."

Trey sat back down, red-faced and aware that Velma was enjoying the fact that the spotlight was, for the moment, off her. "But..."

"And what was that stuff about you being blind?"

"Oh, that...well, I told them I was very short-sighted, which was why I couldn't find the washroom. Except what I *said* was that I had a bad case of myopia, which Mr. Cavallo took to mean I was sick with something."

"That why he was looking at you strange?"

"Yeah."

"Quick thinking...but lucky."

"Why's that, Dad?" Velma, it seemed, was not ready to let Trey off the hook just yet.

"Because, if Cavallo figured he was being eavesdropped on he'd have been one unhappy *capo*." Mr. Pisbo sat back to let a waiter put a steaming plate of lasagne in front of him. "You seem like a smart kid, Trey, but in future you'd probably do better to think about what you're going to do *before* you do it."

"Look before you leap, right, Dad?"

"Which could also apply to answering telephones," said Mr. Pisbo, with a completely straight face. "Right, Velma?"

Resolutely looking anywhere *but* in Velma's direction, it took all the strength Trey possessed to stop himself from smiling. Or snorting.

"Soon as I finish this, young Mr. MacIntyre," Mr. Pisbo forked up some lasagne, "I'm running you back home, before you can get into any more trouble..."

15 MAKING PLANS

The Royal had in all likelihood, even in its heyday, never been what you could call a Five Star joint, but it was cheap, reasonably clean and had a coffee shop. It would do, and Joe Cullen had booked two rooms for them; he was not doubling up with Dewey as not only could Mr. Dunne afford the expense, but the boy snored like a hog with a sinus condition.

The hotel did not have phones in the rooms, but there were two booths in the lobby and, having sent Dewey to get him an evening paper, Joe took one of them. Closing the folding door, he gave the operator Bowyer Dunne's private number, placed a collect call and waited for it to go through. As he sat on the fold-down chair, Joe lit a cigarette, shook his head and thanked his lucky star that Dewey's little stunt with the boy on the street hadn't ended up with them under arrest on some heinous Federal charge. While he wasn't above a little breaking and entering in the line of duty, he did, however, balk at kidnapping.

"Joe?" Bowyer Dunne's voice barked in Joe's ear. "There a problem?"

"No, Mr. Dunne."

"You got that film yet?"

"Not so far, Mr. Dunne."

"Why not?" Bowyer Dunne's voice rose a pitch or two. "Is there some kind of problem? What is it?"

"There's no problem, boss." Joe tried to sound as calm as possible. "Security at the building's on the tight side is all."

"You call me collect to tell me that?"

"No, I called to say that we should be back tomorrow. Just keeping you in the picture, like you asked."

"In case it had slipped your mind, me being *in* the picture is what this is all about, Joe! Just do the damn job and get yourself and the boy back here to Topeka!"

The phone went dead and Joe was left listening to

the purr of a dial tone. He put the receiver down, stood and exited the booth. Sometimes – no, he thought, make that often – he wondered why he didn't quit and go home to Tampa. Of course, Bowyer Dunne paying quite so well as he did meant the decision was not an easy one.

Joe went over to the coffee shop, which had an entrance from the hotel's lobby; frankly, a cold beer, whiskey on the side, was more what the situation called for, but Prohibition had put an end to a man being able to buy himself a drink without breaking the law. It had also stopped you propping up a bar while you waited for someone, which was why the Royal was attempting to make up for some lost income with a coffee shop.

The only advantage was that, sitting in a window booth, Dewey would be able to spot him without too much trouble; Joe did not want to give the boy an opportunity to get anything else wrong. It was a liability having him here, but Joe hated to think what he might get up to left to his own devices. Which was why he couldn't leave him at the hotel tonight when he went back to the Tavistock.

Dewey had, naturally, managed to get lost on his way back with the paper, a situation not helped by the fact that he'd also forgotten the name of the hotel. A Western Union telegram delivery boy had eventually brought Dewey into the coffee shop, and Joe felt obliged to tip the kid a quarter for his troubles, part of him wishing he hadn't had to take delivery of this particular sorry item.

Sitting watching Dewey chow down on a couple of hamburgers and a soda, Joe made up his mind that the boy had had his chance – not to make too fine a point, a *lot* of chances – and, whatever Joe's wife said, he was going to let him go when they got back. Enough was definitely enough.

"Okay..." Joe waited until Dewey had finished cleaning ketchup residue off his plate with his forefinger, then signalled for the check. "We have work to do, before we go to work."

The old guy running the elevator – "Lester", according to the name embroidered on his threadbare jacket – was fast asleep when they exited the coffee shop and, as they were only on the second floor, Joe elected to walk up.

"What work we have to do, Joe?"

"I have to go over everything that's going to happen tonight, so you know what to do and get it right when it comes to doing it. Mainly you just have to listen to me talk."

"That's it? I gotta listen, is all?" Dewey sounded more than a little disappointed.

"There's slightly more to it than that..." But, Joe thought as they reached his room and he unlocked the door, not a whole lot.

Letting Dewey in first, Joe paused and checked his watch under the hallway light: 9.30 p.m. Three some hours before the main event. Surely enough time to drum a few simple instructions into Dewey's thick skull. Closing the door behind him, Joe slipped on the security chain, thinking what little good it would do in the event of anyone seriously wanting to get into the room. Joe crossed over to the bed, on which lay the package he'd picked up earlier in the day.

"What's in the parcel, Joe?" Dewey sounded excited, like a kid at Christmas.

"You like dressing up?" Joe got his bone-handled clasp knife out, cut the string and stood back. "Take a look."

"Dress up as what?" Dewey came over and unfolded the brown paper to reveal a peaked hat sitting on top of a jacket and trousers. "A doorman?"

"No, Dewey, the maître d' in a fancy restaurant – what's it look like? It looks like a *cop's* uniform, see the brass doohickey on the hat? Know why?" Joe didn't wait for an answer. "Cuz it *is* a cop's uniform, that's why."

"Just the one? What're you gonna be wearing?"

"Me? What I'm standing up in." Joe reached into his breast pocket and flipped open a leather badge holder. "As *I* am the plain-clothes detective, and *you* are the patrolman that's assisting me in my endeavours."

"Are these for real?" Dewey picked up the hat and put it on; it was slightly large and sat a bit low down on his ears, but Joe figured it would do for what was needed.

"Indeed they are."

"Where the heck you get them, Joe?"

"In this city, you know the right people, you can buy anything or anyone. And I happen to have the money and know the right people."

"What if we get caught?"

"The idea is, with you in that uniform, there should be a whole lot less chance of that happening."

"This legal, then? Me wearing a cop uniform and all?"

"No, Dewey, it ain't. Not one bit. But then neither is anything *else* I got planned for tonight..."

16 BEANS ARE SPILLED

Although he hadn't shown it, Alex had been beside himself since they'd left the house, sitting in the back of the Packard with his mother, Davis driving. What was he going to do about Trey? In the car there was not a thing he *could* do, but maybe when they got to wherever it was they were going, maybe he could call the apartment again, see if Trey had come back.

But what if he hadn't? What then? Would that mean those two guys had managed to get Trey, the way they'd gotten him? And how would he know if it *did* mean that?

Who should he tell? Ought someone to call the police?

This last thought made Alex stop chasing his tail for a moment.

He was not a stupid kid (he knew that without anyone having to tell him) and he'd known since forever that there were two sides to his father: the side that he saw at home and when they went places as a family – the friendly guy who shook hands a lot – and the other side. The one that had to do with Uncle Mario. Alex mainly ignored that stuff, but figured it meant his dad would not be particularly happy about calling the cops. That other side was also one of the reasons why he generally went by the name Little, instead of his real name, Klein. This was also so no one would know straight out they were Jewish, which Alex recognized could be a problem in certain circles.

"Where *exactly* we going, Ma?"

Alex's mother, in a pool of light from the rear reading lamp, looked up from the periodical she was flicking through. "Fox Lake, sweety-pie...your Uncle Mario has taken a big house out there and, like I said, we've been invited. I just hope the place isn't too draughty."

"How far is it?"

"I have no idea, sweety. Davis?"

"Yes, ma'am?" The chauffeur glanced up at the rear-view mirror.

"How far is it, this house at Fox Lake?"

"Forty-five, forty-six miles; only about twenty miles to go now, ma'am."

Alex sat forward on the bench seat. "You been there before? What's it like?"

"I've not been there, but Mr. Kl – Mr. *Little* told me it was quite a spread, big avenue leading up to it, stables and suchlike. An estate, he said."

"Why's Dad not with us, Ma?"

"He's already there, dear. There was a meeting and he went down this morning."

Alex, who hadn't turned his light on, returned to the unlit gloom of his corner of the back seat, still with no idea what he was going to do about Trey. He should not be on his way to this Fox Lake place for the weekend, he *should* be back in Chicago trying to warn his friend that he was in danger!

Unlike Alex, Trey didn't come from a world where families had bodyguards the way other people had maids. He looked at the back of Davis's head, his chauffeur's hat on at a jaunty angle; it might look like all he did was drive the car, but Alex knew there was always a loaded pistol in his shoulder holster. This was the first time he'd thought about that not being normal...

* * *

Half an hour later, Davis turned the Packard off the road, its headlights picking out tall, red-brick pillars with stone eagles on top, and fancy wrought-iron gates as the car swept round onto a wide gravel drive.

"At last!" said Alex's mother.

Alex looked at the massive, baronial-style house at the end of the drive. A couple of other big cars were parked outside, and someone was getting out of one of them.

"Looks nice, I have to say," said Alex's mother, gathering her possessions together. "Like it should be in Scotland or somewhere."

For Alex the next half an hour was a blur of introductions, social niceties, a short tour of the house – which was extensive and featured a lot of dark wood everywhere – and finally a few minutes alone in his room. Correction, his suite. He had a bedroom, a sitting room and a bathroom and two telephones. By the time he got there, Alex found that his valise had arrived before him and been unpacked.

He stood frowning at the telephone on the nightstand by the bed. Maybe he could try phoning Trey's apartment again, find out if he'd come back. Or that he hadn't. Alex shook his head; he knew *exactly* what he had to do, and that was to go and find his father and tell him everything that had happened. He would figure something out.

Alex hurried along the corridor to the double staircase that led to the large, semicircular lobby, skidding to a halt as he got there. At the bottom of the stairs, standing talking to a woman in a shimmering silver dress with a scooped back, was the man he'd seen posing on his own by Uncle Mario's car in the photo Trey had taken! Same smile, same slicked-back hair that the man now smoothed down with both hands.

Alex carried on down towards the lobby, scrutinizing the man as he went to make sure he hadn't made a mistake. By the time he'd reached the last stair he was completely positive. Alex watched him light the woman's cigarette with a gold lighter, then saw him lean forward and say something to her; she half-turned and glanced his way, smiling, her eyebrows arched. Alex, realizing he'd been caught staring, turned away, looking for an escape route.

"I know you, son?"

Turning back again, Alex shook his head. "No, sir."

The man frowned as he examined Alex, up and down. "Wait a second – you Nate's boy, Nate Klein?"

"Ah, yes sir..."

"You sure are the spit of your dad, but I suppose you know that already." The man grinned at Alex. "What's your name."

"Alex."

"Good to meet you, Alex, I'm Tony Burrell. It was me you were eyeballing, right? First I assumed it was that young lady I was talking to who'd caught your attention; you near enough fell down the darn staircase!"

"Yeah, see...it's like this, I think you know a friend of mine." Alex felt he could trust this person because everybody in this place was there for one reason: Uncle Mario trusted them, which he knew could not be said of very many people.

"I do? And who might that be?" The man looked mildly puzzled.

"He's called Trey, Trey Drummond MacIntyre III."

"Well, I think I'd remember a handle like that, and I don't believe I do, son."

"He took your picture."

"He did?" The man raised a curious eyebrow. "Where?"

"I'm not sure, but you were right next to Uncle Mario's Duesenberg at some party; he has a shot of Uncle Mario, too."

"Is that right – he with a lady?"

"Yes, sir."

"And who'd you say this kid was?"

"His name's T. Drummond MacIntyre III, and he's at the same school as me, Mount Vernon Academy, the place I go to now we're in Chicago. He's kind of a new friend…and the thing of it is, mister, I think someone's after him! Fact is, they may have already got him…"

Alex hadn't meant to blurt out everything, but this man, being the person in Trey's pictures and a friend of Uncle Mario's, didn't seem like a complete stranger.

"You don't say…" The man pulled on his lower lip.

Alex couldn't tell if he was being taken seriously or having his leg pulled. "It's true, mister, they grabbed me first by mistake, which is how I know."

"They did – when?"

"Today, this afternoon, on my way home from his apartment."

"Your parents know?"

Alex shook his head. "My dad's been here all day and I haven't seen him yet, and my ma would've had a conniption fit and put me back on the first train to New York if I'd told her. It's her worst nightmare."

"Come on." The man indicated Alex should come with him. "You and me better go and get this sorted out, Alex."

The room was quite large, but felt cramped as it was full of over-stuffed leather furniture, a lot of gloomy portraits in heavy gilt frames on the dark wood-panelled walls, and people. Everyone seemed to have fired up a cigar, and consequently the ceiling looked three feet lower than it was because of the cloud of smoke that hung in the air.

Alex was sitting on a leather upholstered dining chair that had been brought in specially for him, and there were seven men in the room, three of whom he knew: his father, Tony Burrell and Uncle Mario. The others he'd never seen before, and so far hadn't been introduced to.

Nervous at first, Alex soon got into the swing and laid out the whole story, from developing the film and seeing the pictures to the kidnap on the street and his eventual release.

"You did good, kid." Mario Andrusa turned to Alex's father. "He did good, Nate. I am impressed with the recall and his cool head. Especially not worrying Esther and waiting till he got up here; shows character." Mario looked back at Alex. "You are a credit to your father, Alex, and let me tell you, the only bad thing *he* ever did was not to be born Sicilian."

Everyone in the room laughed, no one more so than Mario himself.

"Now, about these pictures." The smile disappeared from Mario's face. "I was in them?"

"In one I saw." Alex nodded. "With some guy dressed up as a cowboy, and a lady."

"Right…" Mario's eyes narrowed and his whole body visibly tensed, which anyone who knew him would realize was not a good sign.

"Mario…" Nate Klein stepped closer to his son and put a protective hand on his shoulder. "We can handle this."

"We can?"

"Sure." Nate looked down at Alex. "Remind me, what did you say were the names of these two *meshugenah* who did this terrible thing to you?"

"The one was Joe, he was the boss, and the other he called Dewey." Alex's eyes flicked between his father and an unnaturally still Uncle Mario. "It was the guy called Dewey's idea, Dad; the other guy shouted at him that I was the wrong person, and that anyway it was the film they were after."

"Joe Cullen?" Alex's dad looked at Mario, who raised both eyebrows in silent assent. Nate Klein stood up and paced the floor, hands in his trouser pockets. "And this friend of yours from school, Alex…what's his name again?"

"It's T. Drummond MacIntyre III, but he goes by Trey."

"MacIntyre…" Nate Klein frowned. "We know that name, Mario?"

Mario Andrusa nodded. "I think we do. Kid must be the grandson of the guy Dunne has mentioned."

Nate turned back to Alex. "And you're worried these two men are going to go after him?"

"I figured." Alex nodded.

"That worthless, lying piece of – Dunne told me he had those pictures!" Mario stood up, rigid with anger. "He said he'd got rid of them!"

"And now we know he hasn't," Nate Klein went and stood in front of Mario, looking him straight in the eye, "we can do something about it, right?"

"What d'you suggest?" Mario, somewhat calmer, relit his cigar and sent a plume of smoke up to join the swirling cloud above him. "You think Dunne's got some plan we don't know about?"

"That's a good question, Mario."

"The fact I don't know the answer to it makes me worry. And as you know, I do not like to worry." Mario pointed his cigar at Tony Burrell. "Tony, get on the line, talk to someone back in the city. Say we need eyes on the kid's building – what's it called, Alex?"

"The Tavistock, they have a duplex on the tenth floor, Uncle Mario."

"Right, the Tavistock. Get a patrol car to keep tabs on the area, Tony, maybe an unmarked car outside, too. I don't want Dunne's people in that building."

"You're calling the cops!" Alex could hardly believe what he was hearing.

Mario tapped cigar ash into a polished brass tray. "Not *the* cops. *Our* cops. You want things done your way, you gotta pay for it in this life, *ragazzo*; most especially when it comes to law and order."

"But what if those guys have already snatched Trey?" Alex looked from his father to Mario.

"That is why *I* have to make a call as well, Alex." Mario snapped his fingers. "Someone get a phone over here, and find me that rube Bowyer Dunne's number down in Topeka. I think we should invite him to get himself up here PDQ, so he can explain to me, himself, what is up."

"You want the licence plate of those guys who picked me up, Uncle Mario?" Alex dug out a piece of paper from his trouser pocket.

Mario held out his hand, smiling broadly. "You," he said, taking the slip of paper, "are an operator!"

"Come on, son." Nate Klein beckoned Alex over to him. "I should get you back to the party before your mother begins to wonder where you are."

"You mad at me for walking home on my own? It was only a few blocks...and don't get mad at Davis, either, I told him not to come get me."

"I'm not going to get mad at anyone," Nate patted his son's shoulder, "except the damn fool whose fault this all is. Okay?"

"Sure."

"Now go and get yourself something to eat," Nate ushered Alex out of the room, "and I'll be along in a couple of minutes."

Closing the door, Nate went back over to where Mario was sitting.

"Apologies if I might've scared Alex." Mario took a sip of his whiskey. "He okay?"

"He's fine."

"That motto: sticks and stones may break my bones? I can deny anything anyone *says* about me, Nate, but you know I can't afford for there to be pictures. If the old man were to see those..." Mario started pacing up and down. "What d'you think Dunne's up to?"

"We won't know until he tells us, Mario." Nate watched his friend and business associate, thinking how many times he'd told him to be careful, warned him that being married to the boss's daughter meant there were rules he absolutely should not be caught breaking.

"This whole thing feels off...too many coincidences all the way down the line."

"You mean, like the kid with the camera turning out to be some Democratic party bigwig's grandson?"

"Exactly like that, Nate...I mean, what're the odds?"

"Not the kind I'd like to bet on."

"Me either." Mario got out a small lacquered penknife and began cleaning his fingernails. "Although I'd put good money on Bowyer Dunne regretting he ever lied to me..."

17 MIDNIGHT OIL

Fred Pisbo pulled up outside the front entrance to the Tavistock and looked over into the back of the car. "Here you go, Trey: door-to-door service."

"Thanks for the ride, Mr. Pisbo...and for the dinner and all."

"My pleasure..."

"Actually, Dad, the pleasure was *all* mine. I had someone who made *conversation* and didn't just grill me about my grades." Velma, in the back along with Trey, leaned across him and peered out of the window.

"Nice place. Doorman and *every*thing – not all yours, is it?"

"No..." Trey shifted so he wasn't quite so close to Velma. "You want my number, Mr. Pisbo, so's you can call me tomorrow and let me know what you've found out?"

From nowhere Velma had a notepad and pencil to hand. "Give it to me, Trey, that way it won't get lost."

"Oh, right...okay." Trey glanced at Mr. Pisbo, who gave a resigned nod. "It's Clark 2-7400."

"2-7-4-0-0." Velma scribbled for a couple more seconds, then tore a page out of the notebook with a flourish. "And here's our out-of-hours number, Mr. MacIntyre!"

"Velma..."

"Okay, Dad – goodnight, *Trey*, and remember..."

"I know, 'look before you leap'." Trey picked up his satchel and opened the door. "Goodnight, Velma, and thanks again for taking on the case, Mr. Pisbo."

"Pleasure's all mine – I'll speak to you tomorrow, Trey." Mr. Pisbo shifted the car into gear, waited until Trey had shut the door and accelerated away.

In the back window Trey could see Velma waving at him and he couldn't stop himself from waving back. He turned, saw the night doorman, Nestor, was watching him from the foyer, and stopped. Nestor, who only opened doors for people who were likely to tip him, stayed where he was and let Trey find his own way in.

"Cute," he said, as Trey walked past.

"We're just friends," Trey replied, making for the elevators.

As the elevator doors closed in front of Trey an unmarked Detective Squad Nash LaFayette sedan pulled up and tucked itself into a parking space diagonally opposite the Tavistock. The driver, a newly appointed officer called Mahey, killed the lights, put the brake on and switched the engine off.

"We here *all* night?" he asked his companion, an older man.

"Think of the untaxed overtime, kid." The other detective, Sergeant Lynott, pulled the brim of his hat down over his eyes and leaned his head against the window. "I know I am."

"What're we supposed to be looking for?"

"*You* are supposed to be keeping an eye on the place. *I* am getting some shut-eye. Only wake me if anything untoward happens."

"Unto-what?"

Sergeant Lynott rolled his eyes, which Detective Mahey couldn't see because of the hat. "You see any trouble, you wake me, okay?"

"Sure, but—"

"Listen, Mahey," Sergeant Lynott pushed his hat back and sat up. "Learn this lesson and learn it well: jobs like being asked nicely to watch this building, ones we do 'under the counter', if you get my drift, you *never* ask questions about. You do them, you take the money and you keep your lip buttoned. I can't trust you to do that, I'll have you reassigned in a heartbeat."

Detective Mahey watched his partner settle back down, thinking it would probably be best if he left the conversation at that; in the short time he'd been with the Department he'd realized that curiosity about the wrong things was not appreciated. He might be new to the job, but he wasn't wet behind the ears, and he knew that an "under the counter" job meant one that wasn't real police business. Someone was paying to have it done, and more than likely paying with Mob dollars. When gang bosses like Al Capone virtually ran the city, what else did people expect? And anyway, all they were doing tonight was keeping an eye on an apartment building, which was hardly a crime.

Sitting back and cracking open the window slightly, Detective Mahey looked at his watch: just after ten o'clock. It was, he thought, going to be a long, dull night. This part of town, nothing much happened, so what made *this* place they'd been sent to watch so special he had no idea. Then he saw a Ford Model A police patrol car come up the street; watching it slow right down as it drove by the front of the building he realized they must've been sent to do a check as well. As the Ford drove away he made a mental note of the number on its door – 135 – and wondered who the heck could be worth this much attention.

The apartment was very quiet when Trey got back. Nella the maid was in her room; she hadn't left a note saying his friend Alex Little had called because she'd never been taught to write, and had forgotten to tell Cook. Trey's mother was already asleep, having come home earlier with "something of a headache", according to Cook, and taken herself to bed. When he got upstairs Trey himself did not feel remotely tired, in fact *his* head was a-buzz with everything that had happened since he had come back from school with Alex.

Sitting down at his desk he got a pencil and a notepad and decided to write it all down in as much detail as possible, then copy it out again neatly, in pen, and file the end result. That had to be, he was sure, what Austin J. Randall would do.

When he'd finished, having had to redo a couple of pages because his pen had leaked blots all over the place, Trey decided that the next thing he definitely needed to get was a typewriter – a thought that reminded him of Velma, her green eyes and very straight fringe. And her smile. Trey hurriedly checked the time and was amazed to find that it was 11.30 and he *still* wasn't at all sleepy.

Feeling that he should do something constructive, Trey dismissed the idea of clearing up his room and instead decided that printing the rest of the film – plus making new prints of the pictures he'd left with Mr. Pisbo – was the thing to do. Rolling up his sleeves, Trey went to work and, an hour later, he had an impressive array of 5x4-inch black-and-white prints clipped up to dry on the line that hung over his bath.

Standing back to admire his handiwork, Trey had to admit that now he did feel like going to bed, though he was also a tad hungry. What he definitely needed, in the form of a nightcap, was a glass of warm malted milk and a cookie. He switched the light off in the bathroom and made his way downstairs. There was *always* a ready supply of Cook's melt-in-the-mouth shortbreads and her amazing cinnamon-and-raisin cookies in the larder.

As he turned the corner to go down the passage that led to the kitchen, Trey noticed there was light coming from underneath the door and figured Mrs. Cooke must've left it on by mistake; so, when he pushed the swing door open, it was something of a surprise to find Cook at the pine table, in her voluminous nightgown, a lacy cap covering her grey hair. The table was littered with ingredients – butter, various packets and tins, jars of dried fruit – and the air had a faint mist of flour in it.

"Mister Trey…" Cook wiped her hands on her striped apron. "What you doing up this late?"

"What're *you* doing cooking so late?"

"I have insomnia, Trey, always have. Well, ever since Mr. Cooke died, which now seems like forever ago to me. I find baking helps settle me. What you looking for?"

"A glass of malted milk and a cookie. I've had quite a day today, and I think *that* would settle *me*."

"Got a better idea…" Cook went to the sink and rinsed her hands under the faucet, looking over her shoulder at him. "How does a mug of hot *chocolate* and a cookie sound?"

"Like a *much* better idea!"

Detective Mahey checked his watch again. It was just after half past midnight; only five minutes since he'd *last* checked the time. He'd been absolutely on the button about the evening so far: duller than a roomful of maiden aunts. About the only thing that had happened, apart from someone taking a couple of small dogs out for a walk round the block, was Car 135 coming by two more times. He glanced at Sergeant Lynott, slumped fast asleep to his right; nothing at all there to bother him with...

18 TICK-TOCK...

"Tony, fold...I need you for a moment or two." Mario Andrusa had walked into one of the smaller, less extravagant rooms in his mansion. Most of the space inside was taken up with a circular, baize-covered table around which five men sat nursing hands of cards and small shot glasses of whiskey.

"Sure, boss." Tony grinned and spread his cards in a fan on the dark green material, then stood up. "Two pair – queens over nines. My hand, I think; cash me out, fellas."

To the sound of general disgruntlement, Tony having won three out of the five previous hands, he followed Mario out of the room. "What's up?"

"Finally got a hold of Dunne." Mario, standing by an oak dresser, held up a cut-glass decanter, half full of a pale caramel-coloured liquid. "Want one?"

Tony nodded. "Over ice."

Mario shook his head and tutted. "This is a single malt, Tony, not some back-room bourbon. A little water, if you must."

"I'll take it straight." Tony accepted the tumbler Mario handed him. "You go hard on Bowyer?"

"I may have yelled." Mario shrugged.

"He on his way?"

"If he could already be here, he would be. That's what he said. He also told me the registration of the car his people drove up in, which was the same as the one Alex already gave us." Mario sipped his whiskey, savouring its taste. "Nate guessed right, it is Joe Cullen, and some kid he took with him."

"Right." Tony put his glass down. "I'll make another call..."

Dewey, in his own room, smaller than Joe's, checked himself out in the mirror above the chest of drawers.

Apart from the cap being a tad on the big side, everything fitted, even the knee-length leather boots, and he thought he looked the bee's knees. Just like a real cop. He particularly liked the five-point star badge pinned above the left breast pocket and wished he had a camera so he could take a picture to show his mom. Dewey turned around and tried to see what he looked like from behind, thinking maybe he *should* seriously consider joining the police. Get a career. He might talk to Joe, see what he thought.

The only fly in the ointment, to his way of thinking, had been that while he might have a nightstick hanging from his belt, the leather holster was empty. But he'd solved that problem by borrowing the spare pistol, a .22 that Joe kept in a cigar box in the glove compartment of the Chrysler. He hadn't asked, as he knew Joe would most probably say no. He'd just sneak it back as soon as the job was over; but with the gun on one side and the stick on the other, he felt he was the genuine article.

As he was adjusting his cap to see if he couldn't make it sit better there was a sharp rap on his door, and Joe walked in.

"You ready?"

"Yup."

"Remember everything I told you?"

Dewey nodded. "It's just this hat…"

"The cap's fine, Dewey, what's important is that you remember what I told you."

"I gotta not say anything, unless you talk to me; I always have to say 'Yes, sir!' to you, when you *do* say something, ah..." Dewey looked down at his boots, then up again, "...and my job is to remain on guard by the door while you're getting the film and the pictures. Right?"

"You do all that, everything'll be copacetic." Joe looked at his watch. "Time we went."

The headlights in the rear-view mirror alerted Mahey to an approaching car. He watched it go past him, slow as it crossed the intersection and then, instead of carrying straight on, he saw the driver do a neat U-turn and pull up outside the Tavistock.

Mahey blinked and sat up, frowning: was this what they'd been waiting for, the start of some trouble? He watched a man get out of the driver's side and straighten his suit jacket, and was about to shake Sergeant Lynott awake when he saw the person in the front passenger seat get out. It was a uniform, the street lights reflecting off his badge. Mahey relaxed. They must both be cops.

The two men walked up to the building; getting something out of his jacket, the plain-clothes cop tapped on the glass a couple of times and then held up what Mahey assumed must be his ID. He saw someone come up to the door and let the two cops in. Whoever lived here must, he reckoned, be very important; or possibly very bad. One or the other had to be the case.

"What's the problem, officer?" Nestor smiled at the taller plain-clothes cop and then the shorter uniformed guy.

"Not sure there is one."

"Oh, really, then..." Nestor looked puzzled.

"We have to check the building."

"At one o'clock in the morning, officer?"

"Crime doesn't work to a schedule." Joe put his Detective's badge folder back in his jacket. "The desk at the local precinct got a call, we got sent out."

"A call about what?"

"That's what we're here to find out."

"I'm not sure I—"

"You wouldn't be attempting to stop an officer of the law in the pursuance of his duty, would you..." Joe glanced at the name embroidered on the doorman's jacket, "...Nestor?"

"Me? No!"

"Good." Joe smiled. "We won't be long, I'm sure it's

probably nothing, but these days you can't be too careful. McGuigan?"

Dewey, who had been following the conversation like the ball in a tennis match, stiffened. "Yes, sir!"

"Follow me."

"Yes, sir!"

"We'll take the stairs, so we don't alert anyone that we're coming." Joe straightened his tie. "Nestor, you carry on, business as usual."

Without waiting for a reply, Joe strode off across the lobby, Dewey right behind him, and went through the door with the sign above that said "Stairs".

"Was I okay, Joe?"

"You were fine, just fine..."

"I think he believed us."

"What's not to believe?"

Five minutes later, Joe more than a little out of breath, they were in the tenth-floor hallway. There was just the one door. Joe rubbed his hands together and blew on his fingers; he had checked the building as best he could from street level and no lights were showing from the windows he could see. It was, after all, gone 1.00 a.m. and everybody, especially the kid, should be asleep.

This was going to be the only chance he'd have of taking a look around the place unhindered, getting his hands on the film and getting the heck out again. His plan was to be in the apartment no more than five minutes. Any longer than that and he was going to bail, as he saw no point in tempting fate.

Joe fished his set of lock picks out of his trouser pocket. He was a mite rusty, but the lock on this door didn't appear to be anything too sophisticated; thirty seconds later and a soft, oiled *click* proved him right. They were in.

"Right, Dewey, here we go – ready?"

"Sure, Joe, what can go wrong?"

Joe didn't want to think of all the many, *many* ways Dewey could foul up. "Tell me one more time."

"I stay by the front door, all official, and tell anyone that comes that we got called and found the place open."

"Good..."

Joe pushed the door open very slowly; like the lock, the hinges were well-oiled and did not squeak. He ushered Dewey past him, went in and shut the door. The darkened hallway was wide with a deep, soft pile carpet, and opposite where they were standing was a chair next to a table with a silver tray on it. Joe pointed, indicating that Dewey should go sit on the chair, which he did; then Joe stood for a moment, listening.

The apartment was quiet, illuminated only by

moonlight coming from a tall window at the end of the hallway, where a staircase led to the next floor. Aware that he was now on the clock, Joe left Dewey "on guard" and set off towards the stairs; if the boy did have the film and the pictures, they were probably up in his bedroom. Hopefully.

The carpet deadening his footsteps, Joe was up on the next floor in seconds, looking down a corridor with three doors off it. He went to the first one and tested the handle. No noise. He started opening the door and saw pale yellow light and his heart skipped a beat – was someone awake? He waited for evidence they were, but none came so he moved the door just enough to get his head through and take a look.

A woman was lying in a large double bed, hair spread out on the pillow like it'd been arranged by someone, her eyes covered with a pink silk sleep mask; she looked as beautiful as a painting in the low light cast by a bedside lamp that hadn't been turned off. Joe closed the door and went to the next one, which opened to reveal an empty room; the third, at the end of the corridor, had to be it, then...

Downstairs, Dewey was, as he'd been firmly instructed, still sitting in the chair in the dark hallway. He had, though, taken the pistol out of its holster and was imagining that he was a real cop and had just walked in on a robbery, surprising the guys doing the hold-up. Peering down towards the staircase – no sign of Joe yet – he stood up, as that seemed more realistic, stuck the gun out and whispered "Hands up!", grinning to himself. His daydream was interrupted by an aroma that hauled him straight back to his childhood, like he was attached to it by elastic: the sweet smell of baking.

Dewey's saliva glands almost erupted as he recalled his mother in the kitchen, weighing and mixing, greasing pans and sliding them into the oven; he always got given the bowls before they were washed, scraping them with his fingers and licking them clean. Dewey sighed, his right hand falling, and he nearly lost his hold on the pistol.

Unfortunately, as he gripped it tight to stop himself from dropping it, Dewey pulled the trigger.

19 ... BOOM!

Dewey McGuigan stood in the hall, his ears ringing, the acrid smell of burned cordite pricking his nose. For the longest moment he wondered what the heck had just happened.

Upstairs, his hand on the door handle he was about turn, Joe Cullen froze, knowing beyond a shadow of a doubt that what he'd just heard was a gunshot, but unable to figure out who might be responsible.

The other side of the door from Joe, Trey, who had minutes before fallen fast asleep as his head hit the pillow, woke right back up with a start and leaped out of bed.

In the kitchen, busy clearing up so the place was ready for breakfast, Mrs. Cooke, whose daddy had shot enough rats for her to know what a .22 sounded like, dropped her damp cloth and reached for the nearest sharp implement.

Down in the unmarked car, Detective Mahey rolled the window open a little further and listened, puzzled as to whether or not the sharp *krak!* a moment earlier had been gunfire. Hearing no cries for help, he decided not to bother Sergeant Lynott.

The only person who was totally unaware anything had occurred – and would remain so until she woke up some nine hours later, refreshed and headache-free – was Trey's mother. Earplugs and a sleeping draught saw to that.

As soon as the long moment was over, Dewey panicked, knowing that he was truly now in the very deepest of doo-doo. But if he thought Joe's reaction was going to be cataclysmic, he was completely unprepared for Mrs. Cooke. She appeared round the corner looking like someone you might come across in only the worst of nightmares.

She came barrelling out of the kitchen, her lace cap askew, nightdress billowing, sleeves rolled up and a large twelve-inch meat cleaver held aloft. She was liberally sprinkled with flour, giving her dark umber skin a mottled effect. A large woman, originally from Charleston, North Carolina, she was protective in the same way a lioness was protective and people did *not* go round firing guns in any house *she* lived in! She stormed into the hallway – her eyes wide, showing white all the way round – bellowing like a beast. Dewey took one look at this devil-ghost, pulled open the front door and went on the lam.

Joe made it to the bottom of the stairs in time to see Dewey disappearing out the door – with the reason why now bearing down on *him* at speed. Behind him, up on the next floor, Joe heard a door open and a boy's voice yelling something like "Are you okay, Cook?" Whichever way he looked at it, Joe knew he was in trouble: he'd be brisket ready for roasting if he let the crazed lady with the meat axe anywhere near him, but there wouldn't be any way out if he went back upstairs.

Strangely, even though he was trapped and had no

time to work out what to do next, a thought occurred to him. Somewhere in the back of his mind he recalled the Math he'd done with Mr. Haskins, all those years ago at high school. Newton's Second Law – "Force equals mass times acceleration" – came to mind, leading him to believe that, if he was quick enough, this big, lumbering old broad might be going too fast to slow down and take a swing at him. So Joe upped and ran.

Thankfully, it turned out that Newton knew what he was talking about.

Making it past the woman unscathed, Joe bolted through the open door, slamming it behind him. He pelted for the stairs, thinking it best he make himself as scarce as pork at a bar mitzvah, because there was no telling how many other people had heard the gun being fired. Even though he couldn't figure *how* he'd done it, he knew in his bones it *had* to be down to Dewey.

Taking the stairs two at a time, wondering how far ahead the idiot boy could be, Joe promised himself, the moment he got back to Topeka, he was resigning.

Trey came down the last flight of stairs just in time to see Cook whirl round and lose her balance as she attempted to cut a slice off the shadowy outline of a man running past her. She missed, the cleaver cutting only thin air, and then landing flat on the carpet, at about the same time as the front door slammed shut.

"Cook!" Trey dropped his Louisville Slugger baseball bat, which he'd picked up as he exited his bedroom; switching on the lights, he ran up to Mrs. Cooke's prone figure. "What *happened* – you okay? Did you get shot?"

"Oh my Lord!" Mrs. Cooke pushed herself into an upright position. "Me? Shot? No, child, don't know *who* got shot, but it sure wasn't me... I heard it, came running and saw someone, looked like the po-leece, in the hallway. *He* had a gun, but took a powder! Ran off instead of staying to help, seeing as how *we* were the ones being burglarized. Then I saw the other one, the burglar himself."

"The *police* were here?" Trey helped get Mrs. Cooke to her feet. "You sure?"

"One thing I ain't is blind, young man."

"What do we do, Cook? No point in calling the cops if they're already here, right?"

"I believe I need a couple of fingers of something medicinal before I can think straight." Mrs. Cooke made a face as she picked up her cleaver, rubbed her bruised hip and then set off down the hall at a somewhat slower pace than she'd come up it.

Trey, feeling more awake now than he usually did after a good night's sleep, hurtled back upstairs, threw on a shirt and trousers over his pyjamas, and stuffed his feet in the nearest couple of shoes. On his way back down he picked up his baseball bat and made for the front door. He stopped when he saw the black powder burns around the hole in the carpet, wondering for a moment why *anyone* would want to shoot the floor.

Dismissing the thought as a waste of precious time, Trey made for the door, thinking that *that* particular mystery would have to wait to be solved – whatever was happening now, it was most likely happening downstairs, and he was not going to miss it!

Detective Mahey saw Car 135 coming by again, only this time it didn't go by. This time it stopped right behind the auto he'd seen the other two cops park up outside the Tavistock. Two patrolmen got out and seemed to be examining the parked car's registration plate. One of them checked something in his notepad; whatever he had written down, it obviously tallied with the car as the two men were nodding at each other and seemed quite excited. As Mahey watched he saw the doorman come out of the building, pointing back inside, and he reckoned that it was now about time to join the action, whatever it might be.

"Sarge?" Mahey nudged his sleeping partner.

"What?"

"Something's up."

Sergeant Lynott roused himself, yawning and rubbing his eyes with the heels of his hands. "Better be good, Mahey, I was in the middle of one helluva dream."

Mahey nodded out of the car, in the direction of the Tavistock. "We got company."

"What's going on?"

"I thought you might want to find out."

Sergeant Lynott peered out of the front windscreen, frowning as he saw two patrolmen follow the Tavistock's doorman into the foyer.

"Damn right I do...whyn't you wake me before?"

"Just happened, Sarge."

The two men got out of the sedan, shook the kinks out of themselves and began walking over to the Tavistock. As they went, Mahey explained what he'd seen, deciding, under the circumstances, against mentioning anything about possibly hearing a gunshot. Sergeant Lynott, who would've probably given him hell if he'd woken him at the time, would no doubt now give him worse for *not* waking him.

The two men crossed the road and walked up to the Tavistock's wide double doors, strolling in the foyer shoulder to shoulder. As they approached the two patrolmen, who had turned to look their way as they'd come in, Mahey saw someone hurtle into the rear of the lobby; it looked like another patrolman, and he presumed it was the one he'd previously seen with the plain-clothes guy. Closer up he seemed almost too young to be a cop. This newcomer skidded to a halt, like they did in the funny movies, a puzzled expression on his face. Mahey thought he looked like a scared boy, then he noticed he had a gun in his hand.

"That's the guy!" the doorman shouted, excitedly jabbing his finger. "He's one of 'em, like I told you!"

Instinctively everyone drew their pistols, someone shouting "Drop your weapon!"; Mahey could see that the kid was confused, his eyes flicking about all over the place like the steel ball in a game of bagatelle. But there was something odd about the picture, something not quite right, and it took Mahey a second to work out what it was.

"Sarge, he ain't a cop, lookit the—" Mahey was about to say that the pistol was some .22 pop-gun, not a regulation issue Colt, and that this cop's cap was too big, but he didn't get the chance. The guy, whoever he was, made the very serious mistake of raising his gun, instead of dropping it like he'd been told.

The two patrolmen opened fire.

* * *

Out of habit, Trey had gone straight to the elevator and pressed the call button; cursing his own stupidity, he was about to go for the quicker option of the stairs when the doors opened. The car had been there all the time. He got in and thumbed the illuminated "L" button. The burglar must've taken the stairs, he reasoned, as this was likely not only to be the fastest but also the safest way down.

The elevator started its ten-floor descent. Trey stood in the middle of the car, baseball bat gripped in his right hand, unconsciously tapping it on the palm of his left hand as he tried to figure out what the *heck* was going on. They'd been burgled, that much was obvious; he had seen the intruder with his own eyes. But who had fired the shot at the carpet? And while he could see that Mrs. Cooke charging at you swinging a meat cleaver was a pretty frightening sight, what was a *police*man doing running from the apartment like a total scaredy-cat?

The elevator slowed, steel hawsers squealing on pulleys and counterweights being brought to a halt. There was a couple of seconds' silence, during which Trey thought he heard people shouting, then the doors clunked opened to reveal the scene in the foyer.

It was a tableau, five people caught in various poses and all looking right at him. They were circled round a figure sprawled on the ground in a growing pool of deep, velvety-red liquid. The place smelled just like the hallway up in his apartment had, only more so, as if a lot of fireworks had gone off. It was a moment before Trey figured out there'd been a gun fight, his eye drawn to the bullet-riddled mirrors on the wall, smashed glass like ice all over the floor.

Confused, Trey stepped out of the elevator. The doors automatically closed behind him. The only person he recognized was Nestor, the night doorman, and he noticed that two of the men looking at him were in uniform, just like the person on the floor. The other two were in suits.

The spell cast by seeing the lift deliver a boy, dressed in crumpled clothes and mismatched shoes and carrying a baseball bat, broke.

"Get him out of here, Mahey." Sergeant Lynott tapped his partner on the shoulder. "He shouldn't see this."

"Sure, boss..." Mahey, who had a couple of nephews about this boy's age, put his pistol away as he stepped round the body on the marble floor. "Shooting must've woken him up."

"You tell anyone else you see that everything's under control down here," Sergeant Lynott called after him. "Say we'll be by in the morning to take statements, and there's nothing to worry about, right?"

"Yup." Mahey waved as he reached where Trey was standing, his mouth open, a puzzled expression on his face. "It's okay, kid, my name's Mahey, Detective Mahey." The Detective gently turned Trey away from the scene and pressed the elevator button. The doors opened immediately. He walked Trey into the car. "What floor?"

"Floor?"

"Yeah, where d'you live?"

"Oh…right…the tenth. I live on the tenth – what happened back there?"

Mahey pressed for the tenth floor. "An accident, someone made a mistake."

"Is he dead, the guy, the cop?"

"I don't know. I didn't personally check."

"There was a *lotta* blood."

"That there was."

"Was he the one came to our apartment?"

"You had a uniform in your apartment?"

"Yeah…" Trey shrugged. "He shot the hallway carpet."

"The carpet?" Mahey frowned, realizing he *had* heard gunfire but finding it hard to believe that anyone would shoot the floor. "Was this person by any chance with a plain-clothes guy as well?"

"You mean the burglar?"

The elevator arrived at its destination and Mahey stepped out onto the landing, and looked back at the boy. "Burglar? You sure about that?"

"He's sure, and as sure as the sun rises every God-given morning, so am I, young man! Where have you *been*, Mr. Trey? Had me worrying!"

Mahey turned to see the door to the apartment filled with the imposing sight of Mrs. Cooke, arms folded and looking somewhat dishevelled.

"He's a detective, Cook, and there was..."

"Well thank you for returning him, Detective," Mrs. Cooke butted in, taking Trey by the arm and leading him back into the apartment. "This child has had *more* than enough excitement for one night, and it is *well* past his bedtime."

The next thing Mahey knew, he was looking at the polished brass numbers "1" and "0" on the glossy black paintwork of the front door and listening to the key being turned in the lock.

Going back down to the lobby he wondered if Sergeant Lynott would have any more idea than he did about all this. Nothing made any kind of sense. Including someone dressed as a cop shooting up a carpet.

20 MOVES ARE MADE

Joe Cullen stood in the stairwell, holding onto the banister for support. He felt physically sick, partly because he was an out-of-shape 46-year-old and he'd just run down ten flights of stairs, but mostly because of what was in the lobby.

He'd been a couple of floors away when he'd heard the shots echoing up towards him, and he knew that could only mean bad things were happening. Things that *had* to involve Dewey, as Dewey'd been on the run and would, because he only ever thought in straight lines, be making for the front of the building where the car was parked.

By the time Joe got to ground level he could hear raised voices. He peered through the small window, set in the door to the foyer, and could just see, on the left-hand edge, a uniformed arm on the marble floor, a pistol clutched in the hand protruding from the sleeve. Joe recoiled in shock at the sight of the body. Had to be Dewey; he recognized the gun, the .22 he kept in the glove compartment of the car. The fool boy must've sneaked it out. But who had shot him? Going back to the door, Joe pressed his face against the glass and saw that Dewey – it *had* to be him – hadn't moved; was he dead? Then a uniformed cop, pistol in hand, came into view and Joe moved out of sight.

As he did so he saw the lift doors open and a young boy come out, holding a baseball bat like he meant business. Joe saw the MacIntyre kid at around the same time the kid himself saw what was happening in the foyer, and Joe watched as a look of disbelief and surprise clouded his young face.

Joe stepped back, in case the boy glanced his way; things were plainly not looking good and Joe knew he had to get away, and quick. If he stayed where he was much longer he'd be caught in whatever dragnet the cops had set up around the building – something they were bound to do, as, by now, the doorman would've told them that Dewey had had an accomplice. Although what *real* cops were doing here at this time of night Joe had no idea.

A small part of him did feel responsible for getting Dewey into the mess he was in, but the kid – always an accident waiting to happen – had really done it this time. Right now, though, Joe needed to look after No. 1, which meant getting out of the building ASAP before anyone came looking for him. Joe had served his time in the US Army, and seen some action in Ypres, France, towards the end of the Great War. He knew you stuck by your comrades, and they stuck by you, but he also believed there was no point in being a dead hero. That way, nobody benefitted.

Quickly taking stock of where he was, Joe spotted another door in the shadows at the back of the stairwell. With one last glance towards the lobby, and quickly crossing himself, Joe fished out his police badge and walked over to the door he thought had to take him towards the rear entrance. Anyone he met, he'd be a detective looking for "person or persons unknown" who might've run that way after the shooting.

It turned out the door led to the basement and, it being now well after half-past one in the morning, Joe met no one in the dark labyrinth under the building.

Ten minutes later he was out on the streets, a block away from the Tavistock and walking fast – but not so fast he'd look like he was running from something – in the direction of the Royal.

The *only* person who had known he and Dewey were going to be at the Tavistock had been Bowyer Dunne. Ergo, as his high school Math teacher, Mr. Haskins, would have said, Dunne had talked. Why and to whom there was no way of telling. But something had gone very badly awry and from now on he was going to have to watch every step he took on the way to getting himself out of town *real* fast.

As he walked he dumped the police badge in a trash can and then, separately, his pistol. He was definitely *not* going to wait till he got back to Topeka to resign. He was doing it right there and then. No going back. A few more minutes and he made another decision: he wasn't just going to stop working for Bowyer Dunne, he would stop being Joe Cullen as well.

Into the next trash can went any personal identification he was carrying. He thought west was the way to go. California. Some place on the coast. Another state, a new name, a new start. Shame about Mrs. Cullen. But if he stuck around, the unhealthy combination of trigger-happy cops and Bowyer Dunne's Mob connections made it more than likely she'd pretty soon be a widow anyway. She'd be safer without him.

All this because some kid had taken a bunch of pictures...

It was 3.15 a.m. when Sergeant Lynott and Detective Mahey finally got back to the station house. You didn't walk away from a shoot-out in the foyer of a ritzy place like the Tavistock in five minutes, like you would if the same thing happened at some south-side tenement. Added to which there was all the confusion about who it was got shot. A boy, hardly started shaving, in a kosher uniform – real badge, boots, belt and everything – who wasn't a cop. Mahey had been right, but he hadn't spotted the gun and the cap early enough, and now the kid was under guard at Northwestern Memorial and it looked like the only way he was coming out was feet first.

There had also been no sign of the partner, the guy in plain clothes Mahey had seen the doorman let into the building, claiming there'd been a call needed looking into. The two men then going up ten floors, breaking into an apartment and screwing the whole thing up when one of them fired a shot at the floor. What, Sergeant Lynott wondered, had these two clowns been up to? Maybe a cup of coffee and a stale donut might help his brain cells work something out.

"Sergeant?"

Lynott looked up from pouring sugar into his mug and saw his captain. "Yessir?"

"A moment."

Sergeant Lynott followed the Captain into his office and shut the door behind him, wondering if the sky was about to fall on his head for what had happened. "I was just about to write it up. The incident."

"Incident?" The Captain, now behind his desk, shook his head. "I heard it was like the Alamo over there."

"Not hardly, Cap. One guy shot is all."

"It's enough. What happened?"

"We're not sure, Cap." Sergeant Lynott, who had been over the story a couple of times with Mahey, so they both got everything straight, pulled out a chair and sat down without asking. "But whoever asked for the place to be watched must've known something was up, right?"

"I hear an apartment got broken into...they get anything?"

Sergeant Lynott shook his head. "Not that we believe."

"You *believe*?" The Captain sat forward. "You didn't check yet?"

"I figured trying to find this second guy was top of the list, Cap." Lynott shifted in his seat.

"*I* make the lists round here, Sergeant!"

"Yessir."

"And top of mine is that you get back to the Tavistock first thing! People like that are apt to pick up the phone to the Mayor if they have a complaint – and the Mayor is apt to listen. Which is when *I* get my ear chewed off..."

21 A TRIP TO THE COUNTRY

Having fallen asleep, his head full of images of what it must've been like to be involved in the shoot-out downstairs – lead flying everywhere – Trey had then spent the night in the middle of tyre-squealing automobile chases and ferocious tommy-gun battles. The dreams were powerful and intense and he was right there, in the shadowy midnight streets of Chicago, collar turned up against the cold wind, fedora pulled down, a silent witness to the lawless mayhem being played out in front of him.

He'd woken early on Saturday morning, around seven-thirty, with the smell of cordite still in his nose, and lain in bed for some time thinking about everything that had happened the night before. Hunger, and a need to discuss these events with Mrs. Cooke, eventually got him up. It was on his way downstairs that he remembered he was supposed to call Velma and Mr. Pisbo and see if they had any news about Alex.

He ran back up to his room and spent a frustrating couple of minutes trying to find the piece of paper with the out-of-hours phone number on it. Eventually finding it in his pocket he hared back down to his pop's study. Velma picked up after a few rings.

"The Pisbo residence, who's calling?"

"It's me, Trey."

"Mr. MacIntyre! And how are you this morning!"

"I'm absolutely fine, Miss Pisbo," Trey said, mimicking Velma's "professional" tone, then dropping it. "You got any dope on Alex yet?"

"Not so far, but Dad was talking to someone earlier, and we're leaving for the office in about half an hour. From what I gather, we're going on a drive somewhere; I heard him say it was a recce, whatever that is."

"A drive, a *recce*?" Trey sat bolt upright; they were going on a reconnaissance mission without him? "When?"

"Like I said, after we go down to the office... Look, my dad's saying something to me from another room. I gotta go, but I'll call you as soon as we get home, okay?"

The phone went dead and Trey's head went into a spin. Mr. Pisbo must've found out something and was going off on an investigation – with Velma, but *without him*! Frozen by a combination of anger and indecision, Trey sat at the desk, the ticking of his father's brass-cased carriage clock loud in the silence. He could not let this happen. Must not. But how?

Sitting staring at a wall of books was, he knew, not going to get him anywhere. Clearly, some action was called for so he stood up; as he did so he realized there was only one thing he could do.

Getting out of the house had taken some doing, even though his mother was still asleep; Mrs. Cooke was, in many ways, a *much* harder person to get past than either of his parents. It had been touch and go at one point, but she now believed he was off with his new best friend, Alex. And he had promised faithfully to be back in good time to get ready for an early supper; his father was due home from his business trip and would expect him to be there.

The whole way downtown on the train he'd fretted and agonized about what he'd do if Mr. Pisbo had already left by the time he arrived at the office. And then, as soon as he'd gotten off and was out on the street, he realized he had no idea what he was going to say to Mr. Pisbo to convince him he should be taken along.

Turning a corner he saw a car was parked up outside Mr. Pisbo's office building, a red Chrysler 50. Mr. Pisbo was standing near to it, looking very much as if he was having an argument with a skinny little man in a shiny suit and a black snap-brim hat that had seen better days. Trey spotted Velma, sitting in the front passenger seat of the car, at about the same time she saw him.

"Mr. MacIntyre!" she said, getting out and coming round the car to join him on the sidewalk. "To what do we owe the pleasure?"

"Hi, Velma..." Trey, too anxious to play games, glanced past her at Mr. Pisbo. "Need to have a word with your dad."

"He's somewhat otherwise engaged," Velma looked over her shoulder, "as you can see."

"What's the problem?"

"That there is Mr. Shady Jones, you might remember my dad mentioning him last night." Trey nodded. "Well they are not seeing eye to eye right now."

"How so?"

"Mr. Jones says as how he got himself down here on time *and* with the requested information – all at no small personal effort on his part." Velma shrugged. "And he then states he needs a ride somewhere, to which my dad replies that he isn't a 'goshdarn taxicab service', words to that general effect."

"Oh..."

"Also, Mr. Jones seems to hold the strong opinion that my dad owes him this favour, and my dad *really* doesn't agree. That's about the size of it; although you'd never guess, the fuss they're making."

"Okay, right..." Trey was getting the distinct impression that Mr. Pisbo was in no mood to answer positively to requests this morning, at which point Mr. Pisbo noticed Trey's arrival on the scene.

"And what the heck are *you* doing here?" Mr. Pisbo stood, feet apart and arms akimbo, staring at Trey.

It was not the friendliest look he'd ever seen, but Trey knew that this was one of those now-or-never moments he'd read about so often in *Black Ace* stories. "I want to come with you...on the investigation. Please."

"What is happening today? Is there a 'For Hire' sign on my car that I have somehow failed to notice?" Mr. Pisbo looked from Trey to Mr. Shady Jones and then at the Chrysler. "No, there isn't. And no, you can't come, either of you. Seeya later, Shady. Now come on, Velma, get yourself in the car, we gotta go."

As Trey saw his chance to go on a *real* investigation – *his* investigation! – go up in smoke, he had a thought, and it was a good one. This was all to do with him and his friend...if *he* hadn't come down to the office and asked Mr. Pisbo to find out what happened to Alex Little – not to mention telling him about Bowyer Dunne, Tony Burrell and Uncle Mario – then Mr. Pisbo wouldn't be about to follow up whatever clues he'd found. Trey really needed to find out if Alex had been kidnapped or not – and if he had he wanted to help rescue him!

Then the cogs in Trey's head clicked into place and he realized that, whatever way you looked at it, *he* was the client...especially as, now he thought about it some more, up on Mr. Pisbo's desk where he'd left it last night was an envelope with $76 and 39 cents of his money in it. A payment in advance. And what was it Austin J. Randall had said about clients in Chapter 21, *Running Your Business*? If he remembered it right he'd said something like "Remember, the client is always right, even when he or she is wrong".

"Excuse me, Mr. Pisbo! May I have a word?"

"Sure, but make it quick, son." Mr. Pisbo, on his way round to the driver's side of the car, stopped and snapped his fingers. "I have to make a move."

The argument had been spirited on both sides (Mr. Shady Jones calling it a "righteous exchange of views"), but in the end Mr. Pisbo was forced to admit that Trey was indeed a client. Which was how come Trey now sat in the back of Mr. Pisbo's car, along with Shady Jones, who had congratulated him on his undoubted moxie for insisting that he, too, got his ride.

"You won't believe what happened last night, Mr. Pisbo." Trey sat forward on the seat.

"Shady told me."

"What?"

"Shooting at your building, right?"

"How...?" Trey sat back in shock.

"Cuz I got *both* my ears to the ground. At the same time. That's how good I am, right, Pisbo?" Mr. Shady Jones nodded at Trey, smiling broadly. "Way I heard it, there was a po-leece gets shot by a *other* po-leece..." Shady shook his head. "Like a Keystone Kops movie, you ask me."

"Wasn't funny at the time," Trey said, not at all sure what to make of Mr. Shady Jones.

"You are going to have to run all that by me again, only this time a bit slower." Mr. Pisbo stuck his hand out of the window, indicating he wanted to turn left. "Cops were shooting cops? That's rich, even for Chicago."

Trey, feeling like he'd had the wind properly taken out of his sails, decided against saying anything about the burglary, in case Shady knew about that as well, and changed the subject.

"So what's this information you got, Mr. Pisbo? What have you found out about Alex?"

"Plenty!" said Velma, turning round and kneeling on her seat.

For the next mile or so, as they drove north-west out of Chicago on a fine Saturday morning, Velma filled Trey in on everything that had happened since they'd dropped him off the night before. In detail.

In the end, it all boiled down to the fact that – "through a variety of contacts and much personal string-pulling", according to Shady – they now knew that various individuals had left the city to go up to a house in some place called Fox Lake. This was, it turned out, where they were now heading.

"So…" Trey frowned, trying to make sense of what did not appear to be very much, "…what about Alex? *Did* he get kidnapped? Is Fox Lake, wherever it is, where they've taken him?"

"Truth is, I don't know." Mr. Pisbo shifted gear. "Shady and I couldn't find even a whisper about a kidnapping…but, if Alex's father's involved with Mario Andrusa, that isn't such a surprise. They'd be likely to keep a *very* tight lid on something like this. But if he has been snatched, then getting him out of Chicago is what whoever was stupid enough to do it would do. It's all the clue we've got and I think it's worth checking. Hence the day trip."

"Okay..." As Trey sat back to think things over for a moment he noticed Shady Jones; he was fast asleep with his hat over one eye. "Um, Mr. Pisbo?"

"Yup?"

"Weren't you supposed to be letting Mr. Jones off somewhere?"

"Dang!" Mr. Pisbo hit the steering wheel with the flat of his hand. "He wanted to get out miles back. Looks like Shady's gonna have a day in the country, whether he likes it or not..."

It was not turning out to be a good start to the day. Neither Detective Mahey nor Sergeant Lynott was feeling particularly chipper as neither had managed more than an hour or so's sleep on a couple of cots at the station, and now they were standing in the hall outside the apartment on the tenth floor of the Tavistock; it was 9.55 in the morning.

Their knocks were answered by the woman Detective Mahey recognized as having shut the door on him last night. Only this morning she was somewhat neatened up. "Excuse me, ma'am..."

"If you came to see young Mr. MacIntyre, you've missed him, officers, he went to see a friend."

"D'you have the address of where he's gone, ma'am?"

"No, I do not. I cook, I keep the house, I don't run a diary service, young man."

"Right..." Mahey smiled, even though he didn't at all feel like it. "Might we come in, ma'am? We have some questions about last night that Mr. and Mrs. MacIntrye, and your good self, might be able to help us with, even if the boy isn't at home."

"Mr. MacIntyre is away and won't be back till later today, Mrs. MacIntyre has yet to come downstairs and," Mrs. Cooke pointed at herself, "it was *me* that was there, saw everything! So you ask away."

"Could we come in, ma'am?" Detective Mahey asked. "Inspect the scene of the crime, see if anything's been taken?"

"Don't think so." Mrs. Cooke looked both men up and down. "You can come back when Mr. MacIntyre's here, if you want; I would suggest after 8.30 this evening."

For the second time, Detective Mahey found himself looking at the brass numbers on the door. He glanced at his partner. "You were a lot of help there, Sarge."

"You should see me when I got a warrant..."

22 FOX LAKE

When Alex finally woke up he could not believe it was well after ten o'clock – almost half past, according to the clock on the mantel. Then he remembered that he hadn't actually gone to bed until sometime after two in the morning. He and the other kid who was at the house for the weekend (a girl, but nothing was ever perfect) had been allowed to stay up, basically until they fell over. He'd outstayed the girl, Arianna Something-or-Other (he hadn't been paying attention) by a good quarter of an hour.

Splashing some cold water on his face and getting dressed lickety-spit, Alex got himself downstairs in no time. On the one hand, he was ravenous and did not want to miss out on breakfast, and on the other he wanted to find out what had been going on last night. Tony, Mario and his father had been in huddles all evening, Tony being called away a couple of times to take phone calls. Whether any of this toing and froing had anything at all to do with Trey he didn't know, but he was determined to find out.

The dining room was empty when he got there, but on the sideboard he found heated, silver-domed platters of everything from pancakes, sausage links and Canadian bacon, to three kinds of eggs and grilled tomatoes. A maid came in and took his order for toast and a glass of orange juice, and Alex was loading up a plate when his father came into the room, dressed casual in tan slacks and a light blue open-necked shirt, with a dark red jumper draped over his shoulders.

"Didn't expect to see you up this early, son."

Alex sat down at a freshly set place at the table. "You either, Dad. What time you go to bed?"

"True to say, not long after you. Long day."

"Dad?" Alex put a forkful of strip bacon down.

His father looked over from the sideboard. "Yes?"

"You got any news about what's happened to Trey?

I know stuff was going on last night..."

"I saw you eyeballing the proceedings, keeping tabs." Nate Klein brought his plate over and joined his son. "Far as I know, there were people on his building, the Tavistock, all night and there'd been no other news by the time I went upstairs. If anything's happened, Tony'll know. I presume you asking me means you haven't seen Tony yet?"

"I've not seen anyone."

"Not even Arianna?"

"Not even." Alex stopped eating. "Why?"

"No reason..." Nate sprinkled salt and pepper on his food.

"What's going on, Dad?"

"Why should anything be 'going on', Alex?"

"You and Mom don't *ever* say 'no reason' for no reason; what's up?"

"Nothing terrible." Nate sprinkled some Worcestershire sauce on his grilled tomatoes, then reached for the mustard.

"You going to tell me, or just keep on putting stuff on your food, Dad?"

"You guys have to take a trip for a couple hours, is all."

"Which guys?"

"You and Arianna, and your mothers. It's nice round here, plenty to see."

"I doubt that. It's country, all looks the same." Alex shook more ketchup on his hash browns. "Why don't you want us here?"

"There's a meeting come up unexpectedly. Let's leave it at that, all right?"

Alex knew his father well enough to know when to stop pushing. From what he understood of the conversation he'd witnessed in the smoke-filled room last night, he'd bet the "meeting" was going to be with the man who'd sent those two goofs to Chicago – the ones who'd grabbed him by mistake. Bowyer...Bowyer Dunne, that's what his Uncle Mario'd called him. By the look in Uncle Mario's eye when he asked for someone to bring him a phone, this get-together was *not* going to be a friendly chit-chat.

"Sure, Dad, anything you say."

Nate, who'd been expecting more of a set-to, glanced at his son. "Yeah?"

"Yeah."

"I owe you one."

"I'll say."

The moment they were informed they were going to have to go on a drive, both mothers put an expensively shod foot down, maintaining that there was no way they were leaving without getting dressed for the occasion; plus, they wanted a hamper containing the wherewithal to have a decent picnic lunch somewhere with a view. Alex had heard his mother say she required chilled champagne, and some caviar at the very least and his dad saying that was fine, it would happen, but could she hurry up?

Alex had used the time to track down Tony Burrell, who he eventually found out by the garages; jacket off, sleeves rolled up, leaning under the raised hood of a dark blue Lincoln Roadster.

"You know how to fix an auto, Mr. Burrell?"

Tony came up from under the propped hood to see who was talking to him. He smiled when he saw who it was. "Morning…" He wiped his greasy hands on a cloth. "You want a piece of advice? Don't rely on other people to know how to fix your things; they more than likely won't be around when you really need 'em."

"I'll remember that, Mr. Burrell."

"Call me Tony."

"Okay."

"Guess you want to know how things are, back in Chicago, right?"

"Did you hear anything?"

"He's okay, your friend. Nothing to worry about."

Alex looked inside the auto, at the polished wood

fascia and the hand-stitched leather seats. "False alarm, then?"

"Oh I wouldn't say that... You want to have a sit in her?" Tony opened the driver's door. "Be my guest."

Alex stepped up onto the running board. "Something happened...what?"

"They caught one of the guys came up from Topeka, the other one got away." Tony looked at his watch. "Look at the time, I gotta go clean up...and aren't you s'posed to be going for a ride with Guido Vittrano's daughter and her mom?"

"Yeah..." Alex's shoulders slumped.

Tony laughed and mussed Alex's hair. "Coupla years or so, you're gonna be doing anything you can to be sitting on the back seat of some car with *that* young lady!"

"Oh yeah?"

"Believe me."

Twenty minutes later, as Davis put the last of the picnic bits and pieces in the trunk of the car, Alex, who had chosen to sit up front, saw a motor coming up the drive and caught a glimpse of a man with coppery-red hair. Mr. Bowyer Dunne. Alex looked across at the mansion and saw Tony Burrell, now in a different suit, waiting with a couple of other men. The welcoming committee, though no one was smiling.

Alex had a pretty good idea why they'd all been sent for a drive: he'd heard stories about how ugly it could turn out when Uncle Mario got mad, and this Mr. Dunne had seemingly made him fit to spit bricks...

23 STEPS ARE TAKEN

While finding Fox Lake had been a breeze, pinpointing which of the fairly numerous large houses thereabouts was the one they wanted turned out to be not quite so easy. Shady, who was less than impressed at being so far from home, now said he only *thought* it was called The Pines, or something like that, and refused to be more exact. Trey had never seen a grown-up sulk before.

As the last thing Mr. Pisbo wanted to do was sneak into the wrong place, quite a bit of driving up dead ends and reversing back down narrow lanes was called for in the search for The Pines. Trey was beginning to think they'd never find it, and the day would've been a complete waste of time, when Shady leaned over and tapped Mr. Pisbo on the shoulder as they drove along a road Trey was sure he recognized.

"Twelve Oaks, Pisbo."

"Say again?" Mr. Pisbo slowed the car down.

"You deaf? I said 'Twelve Oaks', on the gates you just went past a ways back." Shady relaxed, nodding at Trey. "That the place. Knew it was to do with trees or somesuch, like I said."

Mr. Pisbo pulled the car over and stopped. "You *said* The Pines..." He turned round to look Shady Jones in the eye. "You sure about changing your mind?"

"Came back to me," Shady smiled, "soon as I saw the gates."

"Least he remembered, Dad," Velma said. "Are we stopping long enough for me to let Banjo out? He just woke up."

"Sure, but keep him on the leash."

"You got a *banjo*?" Trey gawked, a confused image popping into his head. "On a *leash*?"

"It a darn *dawg*." Shady shook his head. "'Less they's chasing round the track after a rabbit, or whatever, I got no time for 'em. Not me, no sir."

"You have a *dog*? Where?" Trey shot forward. "You never said, where is he?"

"You like dawgs too, huh?" Shady said. "You kids made for each other."

Velma ignored Shady, turning to open her door to get out. "He's been asleep the whole time down by my feet, that's what he always does in the car. Come and meet him, he's a sweetie."

"If he's such a sweetie, why didn't your mother take him with her?" Mr. Pisbo switched the engine off. "It's her dog."

"You know Aunt Selma doesn't *like* dogs, Dad."

"*I* don't like dogs. Your mother ever take that into consideration?"

"He's *no* trouble, are you, Banjo?" Velma pushed the door open. "And he's *such* a clever boy!"

Astonished at the dog's amazing ability to sleep, Trey got out and scooted round to the roadside. As he got there a small pug-faced black-and-white dog, with pointy ears, jumped onto the grass verge next to Velma. "What is it?"

"What it *look* like, boy...a duck?" Shady, leaning out of his window, rolled his eyes. "You leave your brains back at your house?"

"For your information, *Mister* Shady Jones," Velma stood, hands on hips, "he's a Boston terrier."

"Should go back there, you ask me."

"Well I *didn't*."

"Cut it out, you two…"

A couple of hundred yards or so down the road, back the way Mr. Pisbo had just come, the hood of a smart two-tone, dove grey and black four-door Packard appeared from the driveway of Twelve Oaks. This went unnoticed, back up the road, due to the attention being paid to a small Boston terrier.

The Packard stopped while the driver, Davis, checked for traffic. He saw the parked up vehicle, caught a glimpse of some kids and a dog, but thought nothing of it; no one else in the car with him noticed. The road being clear, he then turned left and smartly accelerated away in the opposite direction.

Half an hour later, having packed everyone back in the car and made as much of a circuit of the Twelve Oaks estate as was possible on four wheels, Mr. Pisbo found the kind of spot he was looking for. Pulling off the road, he parked in the shade of some black walnut trees. He had seen all he could from the road (which was, admittedly, not a lot) and knew that the only course of action open to him now was trespass.

But, first things first.

"Time for lunch…" Mr. Pisbo made a thing of checking his watch, "…pretty much at lunchtime, too. Trey, do me a favour and get the couple of bags in the trunk, would you?"

Trey went round the rear of the car, opened the trunk and saw two brown paper grocery bags packed in an old orange crate; he figured so they wouldn't get thrown around during the journey. "Want me to bring the rug as well, Mr. Pisbo?"

The call came back, "Sure, why not."

Trey put a red-and-green plaid rug on top of the crate and picked it up, surprised how much it weighed. He took it round to where Mr. Pisbo was sitting on the running board, next to Shady Jones, on the side facing away from the road; they were watching Velma playing with Banjo. "Big lunch, Mr. Pisbo."

"You brought the toolbox – the crate's full of spanners and wrenches, son!"

"Oh…I didn't know." Trey felt himself blushing, and waited for some clever remark from Shady, which never came. He put the crate down, put the rug on the grass and took out the two paper sacks, revealing the ballast of various hunks of greasy metal hiding underneath.

"You one cheap dude, Pisbo, you know that?" Shady

got up. "Here, boy, I'll get the *tool*box back where it belong, you put the lunch out. Lord know, the *food* no doubt make-do and hand-me-down, too. Bright side…if it ain't fit for human consumption, leastways the *dawg* won't go hungry…"

The food was a perfectly acceptable selection of Monterey Jack cheese and baloney (with mustard *and* mayo) white-bread sandwiches; there were apples for dessert and soda pop to drink – and Velma, it turned out, could belch like a stevedore. It was a skill that, even though he knew it shouldn't, highly amused her father and made him feel inordinately proud.

Once the feast had been consumed and cleared up, Mr. Pisbo had exchanged his suit for a pair of old brown twill trousers, a faded blue work shirt and a worn flat cap. He got a canvas satchel from out of the car and slung it over his shoulder. "I shouldn't be long," he said. "You two stay right where you are and don't give Shady *any* trouble."

"Eh?" Trey frowned. "Where you going, Mr. Pisbo?"

"To have a look at this Twelve Oaks place, see what's what."

Trey looked at Mr. Pisbo, his jaw set in a bulldog fashion. "What about me?"

"You? You stay here with Velma and Shady."

"And why you bringing *me* into this, Pisbo?" Shady, still sitting on the car's running board, leaned back and folded his arms. "You think I'm some kinda *nurse*maid?"

"But *I* should be coming with you, Mr. Pisbo." Trey could feel an important opportunity about to slip through his fingers. "I can be your assistant, help you find out what's happened to Alex!"

Exasperated, Mr. Pisbo grabbed his cap off of his head. "Look, all of you—"

"What did *I* do?" interrupted Velma.

"Nothing, sweetheart, I meant these two." Mr. Pisbo indicated Trey and Shady. "It was *not* my intention to have *either* of you with me today, and, seeing as how it's your own fault you're here, Shady, you can quit complaining—"

"But—" Trey tried to cut in, except Mr. Pisbo didn't give him a chance.

"And don't you give me any more of that 'I'm the client' stuff, Trey." Mr. Pisbo jammed his cap back on and strode off.

And that was it. Under a cloud of disappointment, Trey found himself watching Mr. Pisbo go through the stand of trees towards the wooden fence at the back of the Twelve Oaks estate. Having started to think of himself as "part of the team" the *last* thing he wanted was to be left behind with Velma, Shady and Banjo the dog. He was desperate to find out if this was where they'd brought Alex – not to mention that this was his big chance to see a real private detective at work, for heaven's sake! There *had* to be a way for him to sneak off...

"Penny for them?"

Trey, aware that he'd been staring off into the wild blue, glanced at Velma. "Nothing..."

"Sure."

"You kids wanna play cards?" Shady butted in, producing what looked like a fairly new pack from his jacket pocket. He shook the cards out and snapped them so they made an "angry wasp" sound. "Gin, brag, cribbage...maybe old maid, happy families more your style?"

"Poker, five-card, jokers wild." Velma put her hand out. "I'll deal."

Shady winked at Trey as he handed the cards over. "That Pisbo a *bad* influence, you ask me."

"I didn't." Trey could feel the slow burn of anger and frustration in his stomach.

"Weren't *me* made the rules, boy." Shady started dealing the cards.

Trey knew he should apologize for being rude to

Shady, but he was too cross with himself for letting Mr. Pisbo walk off without a fight...

Fred Pisbo felt he was reasonably fit, for a man of his age, especially since he'd stopped smoking and given up hot dogs, with extra onions, mustard and ketchup, for at least one meal every day. Velma having pointed out that he was running to fat, and would die a lonely, pot-bellied old guy if he didn't begin to look after himself, had been the spur; that girl was downright incapable of pulling a punch.

As robust as he now felt, the fence, at a good seven foot, had been a test. He'd finally gotten over it, with grazed shins and a slightly dented pride, and found himself surrounded by what appeared to be acres of dense, thorny undergrowth. This was a place where thick gloves and a machete would have been a couple of handy things to have about one's person. Which he didn't. And now he thought about it, he'd left his pistol in the car. Instead he'd brought with him a pair of binoculars, a clasp knife, his camera, notebook and propelling pencil; all of which had their place in the world of a private investigator, but not one in his present position.

Edging himself through the overgrown vegetation as carefully as he could, Fred made painfully slow progress, a few yards taking him more than a few minutes. Then the thorns gave way to regular leaves and branches, which he parted and peered through to see a three-quarter view of a big, three-storey house some way across what had to be more than enough rolling lawn to make a complete eight-hole golf course.

"Jeez..." he muttered, getting out his binoculars. "Some place – like a whole damn country club."

Without thinking, he got his notebook and pencil out and started sketching the layout of the place; it was force of habit, something he did because it'd been drummed into him by his very first boss, Jeff Randall, that *after* the event it was a heck of a lot harder to remember things.

Fred noted down the stables and paddock off to his right, the general curve of the grounds, where trees and flowerbeds were, etc. and the shape of the house as he saw it from where he was. Then he carried on through the bushes as quietly as he could so he could get the rest of the view from the other side. About halfway round he stopped, thinking he'd seen movement from the house in the corner of his eye, maybe even the sound of raised voices. Fred was about to set off again when he heard the sharp crack of glass smashing.

Scrabbling for his binoculars in the satchel, it was a moment or two before Fred remembered he'd hung them round his neck; it took him a couple of seconds to find the room where he'd seen the movement and bring it into focus, and when he did he saw a man with a thatch of ginger hair backed up flat against the room's French windows. These let out onto a wide, flagstoned patio, complete with a fancy stone balustrade and classical-style statues. One of the panes of glass, right up level with the redhead's noggin, was broken, and Fred could see shards of glass spread in an arc on the patio.

When you concentrate all your efforts on one particular sense, such as staring intently through a pair of binoculars, the others have a natural tendency to fade somewhat into the background; which was the reason, Fred figured out later, why he failed to hear the dogs.

24 MANY A SLIP . . .

"**Y**ou see what you made me do, Bowyer? You made me break a window. Not to mention a whiskey glass, two fingers of Glenlivet I had brought in from Scotland myself still in it. You know how much that liquor is *worth*, Bowyer?"

"I'm sorry, Mario...I told you a coupla hundred times now how *sorry* I am!" Bowyer Dunne looked like some weird kind of butterfly, arms outstretched, pinned to the French windows behind him. "How was *I* to know the boy was going to get in and take pictures like that?

There was *no way* I could know, Mario, God's honest truth."

"Why did you tell me you'd got rid of those pictures, Bowyer? Why did you lie?" Mario Andrusa rolled his shoulders and stretched his neck to release tension; then, cracking his knuckles, he walked back over to the bar where he poured himself another inch and a half of whiskey. To Bowyer Dunne it looked like a man reloading. "You got some little *plan*, that why you sent Joe Cullen up to Chicago to get them back?"

Mario had a way of prowling when he was angry, a barely contained fury making him twitch as if something under his skin was attempting to get out. Even if you knew, for an absolute fact, that you were not the target of his extreme pique and vexation, it was like being trapped in a cage with a ravenous wolf.

"I didn't mean...I thought..."

"That's the whole point, Bowyer." Mario stopped pacing and looked over at Nate Klein, one of four other people in the room. "Wouldn't you say, Nate? Isn't the whole point that we want to know what Bowyer here was thinking? What he intended to do with those pictures of me? Am I right, Nate?"

"I'd say, Mario. Certainly looks that way to me."

Mario closed in on Bowyer Dunne. "You wouldn't have been in touch with anyone, would you?"

There was a moment's silence, during which the excited barking of dogs could be heard outside, then Tony Burrell slipped into the room, walking straight over to Mario. "The boy'd left by the time the cops got there, boss, out for the day with some friend."

"What about the other two?" Mario glanced at Bowyer Dunne.

"The one in the hospital turned his toes up a couple of hours ago." Tony shrugged. "The other guy's in the wind, boss. No sign anywhere."

Mario swung back, looking at Bowyer like he smelled bad. "See what we're having to do? All the work, the expense? We already gave some very serious moolah to the campaign, Bowyer, now we have to stump up more to fix your mess? That was not part of the deal. The deal was that *together* we get the guy we want in the White House in November – not someone soft who goes and gets rid of Prohibition. Get our man Mr. Hoover in the White House, right?"

"That's what we're doing, Mario..."

"No." Mario shook his head. "No, that is *not* what we are doing. You screwed up, said it would be better to meet down in Topeka, then go and throw some kid's party, where – was it the nephew, Tony?"

"Grandson."

"Right, right...so the *grand*son of some guy who sits

on high-up Democratic committees and who-knows-what-else, *he* comes along, snapping away like he's the Kodak Kid and..."

Bowyer Dunne was finding it extremely difficult to concentrate. His mouth was so dry it felt like his tongue was shrivelling up, but he was also sweating enough that he had a drip on the end of his nose which he daren't move to wipe off. And he needed to go to the men's room so bad that it hurt. But not as bad as he reckoned it was *going* to hurt when Mario had finished with him.

Not for the first time in the last few days, he wished he'd listened to Joe Cullen about the wisdom of having the meeting and the party on the same day; thinking also that it was Joe should be here in this room, taking the rap. After all, *he* was the one broke into the boy's apartment and made a bad thing a whole lot worse! Through the hole in the window made by the heavy whiskey glass Mario had hurled at him, Bowyer could hear that the barking dogs had become even more excited.

"...and now it looks like you have plans for some pictures that could get me in some *big* trouble. What we gonna do about that, Bowyer? Tell me..." Mario stopped mid-question, his attention broken by the incessant, high-pitched yipping coming from out in the grounds.

"What're those mutts up to? They found a fox or something?"

One of the men walked over to the French windows and peered out at his boss's brown-and-white springer spaniels. The pair of feisty hunting dogs had spotted movement in the undergrowth, which, as generations of breeding had taught them, could mean only one thing: game – something to be chased and, hopefully, caught.

"They seen something in the bushes, boss."

"Well get out there and yell at them to shut up with the racket."

"Sure, boss."

As the man opened the door, the movement caused more broken glass to fall out, smashing on the lichen-covered flagstones; a small, crazed-with-fear part of Bowyer wanted so much to make a run for it he almost stopped breathing. Then the coward in him regained control, and he stayed right where he was.

"Boss!"

Bowyer could hear there was something odd, kind of alarmed in the man's tone of voice, and so could everyone else in the room.

Mario, a quizzical expression on his face, came towards the open door. "What?"

"There's some guy!"

* * *

212

In the bushes, the sound of the approaching dogs became too loud to ignore and Fred put down the binoculars, glancing in the direction the noise was coming from. He saw a blur of brown and white careering his way at some speed and knew he'd been spotted. Cursing dogs in general, and all types of hunting dog in particular, he swung round to make as hasty an exit as possible. But the strap on his satchel caught on the stump of a branch; the strap held and the branch bent, first jerking Fred to a halt, then hauling him backwards and causing him to stumble half out of the bushes.

He could see the dogs, now just yards away and beside themselves with delight – which was bad enough as, for all he knew, they were the biting type. Then Fred heard someone yelling that they'd seen him. He did not know who the Kleins, or whatever they were calling themselves, had come to visit, but the chances were that these people would not appreciate a trespasser. With binoculars. It occurred to Fred that this situation could only be worse if, by some hideous twist of fate, Alex actually *had* been kidnapped and his appearance on the scene were to cause something awful to happen to the boy.

Glancing over his shoulder Fred saw a man in a suit, reaching into his jacket with his right hand; as Fred doubted the man was reaching for a handkerchief to mop his brow, this was not a good sign. Yanking the strap loose, Fred dived back into the bushes before things got completely out of hand. What he hadn't realized was that the dogs had peeled off and were now coming at him through the vegetation. The next thing he knew, there were two snarling canines blocking off his escape route. Instinctively, Fred lurched in the opposite direction, which is when someone fired at him.

25 ... 'TWIXT CUP AND LIP

Velma was about to deal the cards for a second game of poker (she had trounced Trey and Shady the first time round) when Trey thought of a ploy. He'd kind of used it before, when he was sneaking into the party at the T-Bone ranch, but there was no reason to suppose it wouldn't work again here. He stood up.

"I need to go to the...you know..." He made what he hoped would look like a convincing I-need-the-washroom face and marched off into the trees; he was sure there was no way Velma was going to follow him, and he'd be very surprised if Shady did anything to stop him. "Back in a minute!"

Trey heard Velma shout something after him, but he ignored her and dodged through the trees, heading in the general direction he'd seen Mr. Pisbo go, stopping only when he reached the fence. Which was a high one, and without a handy ladder it was not going to be easy to get over.

As he stood trying to work out a plan of action, Trey heard a shot ring out from the *other* side of the fence. Mr. Pisbo must be in trouble! Behind him Trey could make out something of a commotion, raised voices, meaning Velma and Shady had clearly heard the shot too.

"You can't stop me, Shady!" Trey heard Velma yell, her voice shrill with panic. "I gotta go find my dad!"

"What you gotta do is stay *right* where you are, missy, like your daddy say!" Shady was trying to sound calm and in charge. "What good you gonna do, running off with a gun anyway?"

Gun? Trey stopped looking for trees with overhanging branches that he might use to get over the fence. Velma had a *gun*?

The sound of someone crashing through the undergrowth caught Trey's attention and he turned to see Velma coming towards him. Sure enough she was waving a gun around as she ran. She was only a few yards away when she tripped and fell. And dropped the gun.

Trey watched, eyes riveted on the pistol as it tumbled in the air, only two questions in his head: would it fire when it hit the ground? And if it did, where would the bullet go? The gun landed with a thud at the same time as Velma hit the dirt. It did not fire.

"You okay?" Trey helped Velma up first, then got the pistol, which he recognized as a .38 Colt revolver, pretty much the same as one Gramps had down on the Circle M. A quick look told him that it was fully loaded.

"What'm I gonna to *do*?"

Trey looked up to see Velma, shoulders slumped and tears dribbling down her cheeks as she gazed at the fence towering above her.

"I've *got* to get to Dad!"

Trey was considering suggesting that he give her a boost up, and then try and find a way to get himself over, when something caught his eye way down to their right. "Quick..." He grabbed Velma's arm and pulled her after him, mentally crossing his fingers that what he'd thought he'd seen was in fact some kind of door.

"Where...?" Velma tried to hold back, but Trey hauled her with him. "What have you seen?"

"If we're lucky, a way in..."

Trey skidded to a halt in front of a slatted wooden door, some three to four feet wide, with a curved top even higher than the fence. It was locked, but when Trey pushed it felt as though there was a lot of give.

"You gonna shoot it?" Velma pointed at the pistol Trey was holding. "You look like you know more about these than I do."

"Wait a second." Trey eyed up the door, stepped back a couple of feet and took a deep breath. "I have an idea."

He stuck the pistol into his belt, braced himself and then ran at the door, left shoulder forward; he was aiming to hit it full force at its weakest point: the lock. And his aim was true. There was a loud splintering noise, and he careened straight through to the other side, almost tripping up and falling over.

"Did you hurt yourself?"

Trey looked back to see Velma staring at him through the open door. "No..." Trey rubbed his shoulder. "Come on!"

Running down the wide path that had been cut through the thick foliage, Trey came to an abrupt halt when he found himself out in the open. Velma stopped next to him. In front of them was the broad, pool-table-green expanse of the massive Twelve Oaks estate, and some way away they saw the unmistakable figure of

Fred Pisbo. There was no doubt in either of their minds that he was in trouble.

Down about a hundred yards to their left – one dog hanging on to his jeans and another the sleeve of his shirt – Mr. Pisbo was making a bad job of running away. Then another loud *KRAK!* as a shot rang out, making them both duck.

"What're we gonna do, Trey?"

Trey was thinking about whether he should return fire, which was, he had to admit, not a *great* idea, when he saw where they were standing and had a better one.

"Wait here, and stay out of sight!"

"But...?" Velma watched as Trey dashed off.

"Where...?" Velma saw he was running towards where a horse was tied to a fence.

"Why...?" Velma frowned, wondering what the heck Trey had in mind as she watched him leap up into the saddle; she saw him lean forward and unhitch the rope reins and dig his heels hard into the horse, urging it to get a move on. The next thing she knew, he was flying past her at a gallop, almost lying flat as he kicked some more with his heels. He was going straight for her dad!

* * *

"You bozos!" Mario slapped his forehead with the flat of his hand. "Don't just stand there throwing lead at the guy – get after him!"

Bowyer Dunne wanted to look round to see what was happening outside, see who they were shooting at, but didn't dare move in case that got him into even more trouble with Mario.

"You, get away from the window!" Mario, who had not forgotten Bowyer in all the excitement, snapped his fingers at him. "Don't want anything *bad* to happen to you, unless I do it myself. Tony, get someone to take him elsewhere until this is all over."

"Sure, boss." Tony Burrell came over and started to lead Bowyer Dunne away.

"You can use the time," Mario stared at Bowyer as he went past him, "to think of a reason why I shouldn't break some of your bones when you come back, instead of glass…"

"Mario." Nate Klein, by the French windows, beckoned. "You should see this."

"What?"

"Whoever's out there has help. Looks like a kid."

This was, Trey knew, a crazy notion, but what could he do? Only he had a chance of getting Mr. Pisbo out of trouble; all he had to do was ride like heck and not get shot in the process. Simple. It would be as if he was kind of charging into battle; an officer in the Light Brigade, like one of Gramps's favourite poems. Gramps read it out so often Trey knew the whole thing just about off by heart...

Half a league, half a league,
Half a league onward,
All in the valley of Death
Rode the six hundred...

As he heard the words in his head, Trey began to wish he didn't recall them quite so well.

Riding low and to the side away from the house, trying to make himself as small a target as possible, Trey hoped that whoever was shooting would think twice about plugging a horse. He was closing on Mr. Pisbo fast, Velma's dad having his work cut out with the dogs and not really paying too much attention to anything else. The horse was a gutsy beast who liked to gallop, and Trey could sense that bringing him round, so he had at least a chance to get near to Mr. Pisbo, was not going to be so easy.

But this horse was a listener – unlike some horses he could mention – and he stopped on request, pulling up neat as you'd like just past Mr. Pisbo. Trey turned him back the way they'd come and swung himself over to the other side. He could see Mr. Pisbo's shocked expression at his sudden, not to say miraculous, appearance, and he could also hear shouting coming from the direction of the house.

"Mr. Pisbo! Grab my hand, Mr. Pisbo!" Trey yelled, another pistol shot ringing out behind him, the bullet sizzling like an angry hornet as it went wide.

"I thought I told you to stay with Shady!" Fred yelled back, unexpectedly free of the dogs, who'd stopped harassing him for a moment, distracted by Trey's arrival on horseback. But, considering his situation, Fred didn't wait for an answer and made a hasty, ill-judged leap for the back of the horse, which failed.

"One more time, Mr. Pisbo!" A quick glance over his shoulder told Trey they were running out of time, luck and whatever else they might need to make a successful getaway. "One more time..."

Fred Pisbo's second attempt, fuelled by a surge of last-moment adrenaline, nearly pulled Trey off; but somehow Fred got up and Trey stayed on, urging the horse into action and galloping back to where he could just see Velma, waiting half-hidden in the bushes.

"Run, Velma!" Trey shouted. "Run back to the car!"

"She here, too?" Hanging on for dear life, Mr. Pisbo tried to look past Trey, but couldn't. "I'm gonna..."

Trey never found out what Mr. Pisbo's threat might

have been. What he heard instead was another pistol shot, followed by Mr. Pisbo screaming that he'd been hit.

"Keep ahold, Mr. Pisbo!" Trey kept on kicking the horse as hard as he could, expecting something bad to happen to him any moment; then, as he slowed to bring the horse round onto the path leading to the door in the fence, it occurred to him that he was slap-bang in the middle of a "shoot first, ask questions later" situation straight out of a *Black Ace* story. Which, when you *were* right in the middle, was a *lot* less fun than reading about it, in his opinion.

A sudden feeling of anger flooded over him, that these people, whoever they were, thought they could get away with acting like that! If they didn't give a second thought to shooting him, what would they be prepared to do to Alex? Without really thinking through what he was doing, Trey dragged the pistol out of his belt and loosed off three or four wild shots behind him as he urged the horse up the path.

Mario got to the window in time to see a horse with two people on it galloping away towards the stables. He saw one of his boys loose off another shot, which, if he wasn't much mistaken, connected with the larger person on the horse.

"About time one of you hit something!" Mario leaned out of the open French window, just as someone began returning fire, rattling off a number of shots in quick succession, no one actually counting as bullets spanged into stonework and smashed windows. Nate grabbed Mario and flung him to the ground as two more people, automatics appearing in their hands, joined those outside, letting fly a few rounds.

Then, silence.

Mario got up off the carpet, a look of utter disbelief on his face. "Who would do this? Who?"

"We have enemies, Mario." Nate stood, brushing himself down, thinking he was glad Esther and Alex were out of the house. "Want me to make a list?"

"What I *want* is those people, Nate...and I want to know who sent them here. Get Tony to take some of the boys out in a coupla cars. Somebody has gone too far."

"D'you think this was cooked up by Dunne?" Nate stopped on his way to get Tony Burrell. "Could be that security guy of his, Joe Cullen, trying to help his boss, right?"

The corners of Mario's mouth curled very slightly. "Bring Dunne with you when you come back, and let's you and me ask him..."

26 CATCH AS CATCH CAN

Velma had watched, frankly amazed, as Trey did the seemingly impossible and rescued her father – while being shot at! Talk about a hero. Then, as they'd made good their escape, she'd seen her father get shot, grabbing at his leg and screaming. It was horrible.

Frozen to the spot, and wide-eyed with amazement, she felt like she was in a movie as Trey did a real cowboy thing and fired over his shoulder. She'd half expected to see a horde of Indians chasing after them, but had come to her senses and turned tail, running after Trey and her father like she'd never run before, feeling completely terrified, overexcited and not a little awestruck by what she'd just seen.

Trey took the somewhat spooked horse along the path towards the open door, the thunder of its hoofs loud on the packed earth. All he could hope was that Mr. Pisbo, who had one arm around his waist, would manage to stay on till he got to the car.

He'd seen Velma just before he'd started shooting and she'd better be right behind him as he was sure they wouldn't have much time to get away. He didn't know what he'd do if she got caught, because right now priorities had changed. The thing was to get as far away from Fox Lake as fast as they could – and get Mr. Pisbo, who was making terrible noises and cursing about his leg, to a hospital. The job of rescuing Alex had just taken a back seat.

The horse flew through the trees on the other side of the fence and it took all Trey's strength to stop him from galloping past the car and off down the road. He managed to turn him, and pull the sweating animal up to face a stunned Shady Jones, who had been getting more and more puzzled the longer Trey and Velma were away and the more guns he heard being fired.

"What you done stole a *horse* for, boy? Sound like we in big enough trouble already." Agitated, Shady was doing a nervous jig, with Banjo, his lead attached to the car's door handle, joining in. "And what the matter with Pisbo?"

"He got shot, Shady, in the leg..." Trey slid off the horse – now intent on clipping grass after all his exertions – leaving a pale Mr. Pisbo behind. "Help me get him down."

"What foolishness *you* get up to, Pisbo?" Shady joined Trey and began helping Mr. Pisbo off the horse, uninjured leg first. "Man, lookit you! Clothes torn up good, big old hole in your leg – who you been in a fight with? Must at least had to be a bear, with a gun."

"Cut it out, Shady." Fred Pisbo put an arm around his friend's shoulder and leaned heavily on him, wincing. "Help me over to the car...and Trey, go make sure Velma's okay, quick! We gotta get a move on..."

Trey left Shady and Mr. Pisbo and ran back through the trees; coming the other way, her legs a blur, he saw Velma and felt a huge sense of relief flood over him.

"Where's my dad?" she yelled. "How is he?"

Trey came to a halt and began running back to the car with Velma. "He got shot in the leg...Shady's getting him to the car...you see anyone following?"

"I don't know, I didn't look." Velma slowed down as

they reached the car and she saw Shady helping her father down onto the running board, his right trouser leg covered with a heavy, reddish-brown stain which had to be blood; she looked like she was about to burst into tears, but at the last minute didn't. "Oh my... Dad, are you okay?"

"It's not as bad as it looks, sweetheart..." Mr. Pisbo did a really bad impression of a smile. "Honest."

"My opinion?" Shady reached into the inside breast pocket of his jacket and came out with a small chromed flask in his hand. "It *worse* than it looks – you want a drink, Pisbo, as *I* sure do."

"What d'you mean, Shady?" Velma ran over to her dad. "Why's it worse?"

"I ain't no doctor or nuthin', but one thing I *do* know, Pisbo here? He don't look to *me* like a man can drive a car..." Shady twisted off the flask's cap, took a sip and handed it to Mr. Pisbo. "And as *I* never learned me how to do it, we in trouble with a big old capital 'T'. Am I right, Pisbo?"

Fred Pisbo accepted the flask and nodded. "'Fraid so."

Trey hung back, his head buzzing with one thought: did he dare? Sure, he did kind of know *how* to drive, but the trouble was he'd never driven on a road with other cars, even back roads such as those here; but on the other hand this was a *real* emergency. He had to take the chance.

"I can drive," he said.

27 ROAD RACE

The Chrysler 50 was a whole different ball game to the Ford Model T pick-up down on the Circle M, but Trey was determined he was going to do this. No matter that he'd stalled once or twice (the clutch on the Chrysler did not need working nearly as hard as the cranky old Ford's) or that he'd crashed the gears a couple of times, forgetting the exact sequence he needed to do things in.

Trey was concentrating so hard on not wrecking Mr. Pisbo's car that he daren't look at the speedometer to see exactly what speed he was doing, but he thought it must be quite a lick. The fastest he'd *ever* driven down on the ranch was 15 mph, which could hardly be called getaway speed, and, now in third gear, he knew he was going much, much quicker than that.

Up front next to him sat Shady who, Trey was all too aware, had his legs braced against the floor, hands gripping the seat like it was a life-jacket and he was on the *Titanic*. Shady was the picture of a man waiting for an accident, an accident he was more convinced was going to happen than anything else in his whole life. His attitude did not instil confidence.

In back, Mr. Pisbo was attempting to staunch the flow of blood from the bullet wound. A cursory inspection had shown it to be what Trey had read was called a "through-and-through" wound, the bullet having gone in and come straight out again. Whether or not it had hit anything vital was not something the stories in *Black Ace* magazine had equipped Trey to ascertain.

Velma and Banjo were back with Mr. Pisbo. After having a pretty good strip torn off her for taking the gun in the first place, Velma was now making herself useful by reloading her father's Colt with fresh ammunition from the box he kept in the glove compartment.

"Are you sure you're gonna be okay, Dad?"

"Completely..." Her father grimaced as he tightened a tourniquet, made of a none-too-clean piece of cloth they'd found in the trunk. "Unless I get shot again – mind pointing that gun away from me, Velma?"

"Sure." Velma did as she'd been asked. "You only have another eleven, no, twelve bullets left, Dad."

"It only takes one to get the job done, as my old boss Jeff always used to say – *ouch!*" Mr. Pisbo grunted with pain as the car hit a pothole in the lane and he was jolted about. "Trey!"

"Sorry, Mr. Pisbo!" Trey, gripping the steering wheel so hard his knuckles hurt, could feel the sweat running down his back.

"You're doing great, Trey, really..."

Shady snorted. "You believe *that*, you must still believe in Santy Claus and the Tooth Fairy."

"Mr. Jones, you are so *mean*! Tell him, Dad!"

"Mean? Me?"

"Will you quit beefing, you two, and let Trey drive?" Mr. Pisbo's voice sounded strained and edgy and everyone quietened down.

"Dad...?"

"I'm fine, Velma...but I'll be a whole lot better when I get to see a doctor."

"*I* be a whole lot better," Shady muttered, "when I get me outta this car."

"Keep this up and I'll have Trey stop and *let* you out, Shady, I will."

Shady hissed and sputtered to himself like a kettle boiling dry, but he stayed quiet, allowing Trey to concentrate on the job in hand, viz, not crashing.

Things had been going quite smoothly for some few minutes when Trey risked checking the speedo. To his amazement, it showed the needle hovering uncertainly around the 45 mph mark; and then he glanced in the rear-view mirror. Coming up *very* fast behind them he saw a sleek, dark red Pontiac, the driver and passenger both wearing fedoras. Although he was well aware that the fedora was a popular style of hat with people other than mobsters, the fact that Mr. Pisbo had just been shot by possible hoodlums whilst trespassing made Trey feel things were about to take a turn for the worse.

It also made him speed up.

Even though there was a sharp bend fast approaching, Trey took the car right over the other side of the road and into the curve, without bothering to slow down even a little. The driver of another car, coming the other way, had to make an impromptu detour onto the verge to avoid a collision.

"What you doing, boy? This ain't no dumb fairground ride!" Shady made a grab for his door handle. "Tell him to let me out right now, Pisbo…think I'll live longer if'n I *walk* back to Chicago!"

"Calm down, Shady!" Mr. Pisbo grunted with pain as he leaned against the pull of the bend. "Trey, what're you doing, son?"

"Behind us…that car…" Trey gritted his teeth and pushed the accelerator pedal down a bit further. "Sure it's following…there's men…in *hats*!"

"He's right, Daddy!" Velma was on her knees and looking out of the rear window. "And I can see four of them!"

"There they are!" Tony Burrell yelled, catching a glimpse of the Chrysler 50 as it disappeared round a bend in the twisty road. "Don't lose 'em!"

The men who'd taken off across the lawn after the horse and riders had missed nabbing them by moments; but as luck would have it, they'd been in time to see Pisbo's car as it disappeared round a bend. When Tony and his crew had come by minutes later, they'd told him what make it was.

It had not taken very long to catch up with the Chrysler. But, just as Tony's driver was about to take a straight line through the corner coming up, he'd had to jam on the brakes and wrestle with the steering to dodge a head-on with some car being driven back onto the road from the verge.

Vibrantly cursing weekend drivers at the same time as he expertly fought the skid, the driver brought the Pontiac under control and, with a squeal of tyres, back into the chase. "Just cos this ain't the city, don't mean you gotta drive like you was on a farm, right, Tony?"

"Sure...but when I said back there not to lose them, I *also* meant, don't kill us in the process, okay?"

"Ain't killed no one yet, Tony," the driver grinned. "Leastways, not in an automobile."

The plain-clothes Bureau of Investigation officer, driving the car which had been coming down the narrow road in the opposite direction, took a very deep breath and blew it out. "Did you see who was behind the wheel of that first car?"

The man sitting in the passenger seat shook his head. "Nearly having two head-on collisions in as many minutes, I was kinda otherwise engaged; who was it?"

"I'd swear on a stack of Bibles it was some kid..." The driver, who had stalled the car, tried starting it up again, the engine finally turning over on the third attempt.

"You pulling my leg?"

"Nope. And I suppose you didn't get a look at the men in the second car either?"

"Can't say as how I did, why?"

"Because, you want my professional opinion – based on me recognizing someone – what we just saw, that was a car chase. You think any place round here has a phone we can use?"

"Back a piece, maybe. Who'd you recognize?"

"Tony Burrell." The driver checked his mirror and began to turn the car round.

"Good spot! I'm sure we passed a house I saw had a phone line…"

"Hey – I can't see 'em!" Velma, still glued to the rear window, cheered. "I think they might've hit that car *we* just missed!"

"Velma, sit down!" Fred Pisbo grimaced, the state of the road – and style of Trey's driving – bouncing him around rather too much for comfort. "There's bullets all over the darn place here – finish loading that pistol and give it to me, okay?"

"I saw my whole *life* flash all in front of me, Pisbo!" Shady shot a quick, squinty glance over his shoulder. "And that ain't a thing a man such as myself *ever* wants to have happen to him…*and*," here Shady shook a finger in the air, in the manner of a politician on the hustings at election time, "*and*, dang if I don't want to negotiate you paying me a sub*stantial* amount of danger money for putting me through this when I should be somewhere else entirely!"

"Put a sock in it, Shady, you're distracting Trey from his driving with all your kibitzing and arm-waving."

"Where do I go now, Mr. Pisbo?" Trey could see a junction coming up and, for all he knew, either way could take them heading straight for Canada.

"We going to hell in a handbasket, that where *we* going!"

"Shady!" Mr. Pisbo, sounding gruff and in pain, grabbed a hand strap as Trey braked. "Hang a right, son, hang a right!"

Trey, who now knew what the expression "he had his heart in his mouth" truly meant, was about to change gear when he checked the rear-view. "Oh no..."

"What's the matter?" Velma leaned between the front seats. "We running out of gas?"

"No – they didn't crash, Velma...they're right behind us again!"

"You keep your eyes on the road ahead, Trey; everything's going to be just..." Whatever it was Fred Pisbo might have been about to say was drowned out by a loud explosion, which turned out to be Velma; figuring that her dad was in no condition to shoot straight, she was hanging out of the window and taking a potshot at the car behind them.

"You get back in the car *right now*, Velma!" Fred Pisbo made a grab for his daughter, but was flung the other way as Trey swerved to avoid another large pothole.

"Don't worry, Daddy, I can handle this." Velma, her hair whipped here and there by the slipstream, looked back over her shoulder. "You just stop yourself from bleeding to death!"

"What *we* s'posed to do about *us* not bleeding, little girl!" Shady, feeling he'd gone *way* past the point where panicking was going to be of any use at all, lit a cigarette, on the principle that it might help calm him down some. "None of *us* exackly *bullet*proof!"

"Did you hit anything, Velma? Did you?" Mr. Pisbo was finding it hard to credit that a situation he thought was bad enough could be getting worse. "Because we don't know *for sure* that those people in that car are *actually* following us, Velma! We don't know that!"

After having to slow down to turn the corner, Trey was beginning to pick up speed again. Not so long ago he'd been feeling a tad miffed because Mr. Pisbo had left him behind when he'd gone off to scout out the Twelve Oaks estate for any signs of Alex, thinking how exciting it would've been to go with him.

Well, his gramps was very fond of telling him that you should be careful what you wish for in case you get it, and now he surely had got some excitement. Lead was flying, he still didn't know what had happened to Alex and his chances of being home in time for an early supper with his father were looking slimmer by the minute...

28 END OF THE ROAD?

The second Tony Burrell's driver had seen the person in the car in front lean out with a gun, he'd momentarily dropped back and gone as far to the left as he could, without driving off the narrow road. The shot had, as he'd hoped, gone wide. "Who *are* these guys, Tony?"

"People in a whole lot more trouble than they were when they woke up this morning, and that's the truth..." Tony Burrell frowned and turned to the two men in the back. "Get the iron out, boys. And aim for the tyres,

I want these types able to talk when we get 'em."

"Did the shooter look like it was a Jane to you?" The driver, eyes peeled, speeded up again.

"The girl looked like a *kid* to me."

"For crying out loud, they'll be *driving* getaways next!"

"This whole thing's looking bumpy – I mean, the guy getting away like that, on *horse*back?" Tony shook his head. "I read *that* in the paper, I'd think they were pulling my leg."

"We're on the straight now, Tony – want me to get closer?" The driver nodded his head backwards. "So the guys can get a better shot?"

"Go for it – boys, you're on."

The two men in back both racked their recently cleaned and oiled automatic weapons, wound their windows down and leaned out each side of the car. Before either man had had the chance to pull the trigger, the shooter in the car in front made a surprise reappearance and fired twice, making them duck back inside as the bullets whistled past.

"You sure it's the tyre you want us to get, boss?"

"I'm sure, boys. Just do it, will you?"

"Wait a second, Tony." The driver jerked a thumb over his shoulder. "We have company coming up behind, and take a look down the road..."

* * *

The driver of the Bureau's Ford saloon could now see the two cars not that far ahead of him; he shifted gear and pressed the gas pedal down harder. He'd dropped his partner at a house a mile or so back so he could call a number in Chicago that was manned round-the-clock by Bureau of Investigation personnel. He really hoped he hadn't got it wrong about spotting the Burrell character, because if he had he was going to find himself on the carpet in the not too distant future.

He'd only been with the new "gangbuster squad" – set up not that long ago by Mr. Robertson Bonner – for a couple of months. This was a big operation that he was *supposed* to be playing a tiny part in, checking activity at the Twelve Oaks estate, making a few circuits with his partner; the job was to report anything they saw back to his immediate boss, who was waiting with a couple of other men at a nearby hostelry. He was not supposed to get involved in a car chase!

And now, what he saw ahead of him down the road was even more trouble...

Things were, in Trey's considered opinion, beginning to get out of hand.

Next to him, Mr. Shady Jones was loudly muttering

all kinds of nonsense about St. Peter and the Pearly Gates and how he wasn't in *any* way ready to meet either of them. Behind him was no better. Banjo was barking fit to bust and Velma was being yelled at by Mr. Pisbo, who had gone beyond angry; she had just done the *exact* opposite of what her father had said and blasted a couple more shots at the car following them, so Trey could see she kind of deserved what she was getting. And, as if coping with all the racket in the car wasn't bad enough, coming towards him, on what had continued to be a fairly narrow stretch of road, was another motor.

Trey wished he could ask someone (someone who knew how to drive) for advice, but Mr. Pisbo was far too involved with tearing another considerable strip off his daughter, who was, apparently, about to be grounded until she turned twenty-one. It looked like Trey was, as his gramps would say, really behind the eight ball and would have to sort out this situation by himself.

"Boy, you driving this jalopy with your eyes *shut*?" Shady had stopped his grouching and was pointing out of the windshield.

"I can see it."

"Good! That good – but can you *also* see that this darn road ain't even *nearly* two cars wide?"

"It'll be okay..." With a car coming up fast behind

him, and another in front, all Trey could think of doing was grit his teeth and hope for the best. The best being that the other driver took to the verge, like he was about to do, so they would pass without incident. The only problem with this plan was that Trey didn't dare slow down, and the verge on his side of the road was quite high. "Hold on, everyone!"

Trey shifted down a gear, braked slightly and turned the steering wheel sharply to the right...

Down the road ahead he was aware that the other driver was taking a similar course of evasive action...

The steering wheel twitched and jerked wildly in Trey's hands as the car mounted the verge, throwing everyone around like beans in a can...

Weirdly, as they sped past the other car, Trey found himself thinking it looked remarkably like a grey-and-black two-tone Packard...

And then he was *sure* he saw a wide-eyed Alex Little sitting in the front passenger seat, and Davis driving...

Finally, just seconds after it looked like disaster was inevitable, Trey was hauling the wheel to the left and getting the car back on the road again. He'd done it!

He wasn't sure exactly *how*, but he had done it!

It looked like everyone had survived as well, although both Shady and Banjo had been rendered silent by the dramatic manoeuvre, while Mr. Pisbo was oohing and aahing that his leg hurt *real* bad and Velma was making a fuss and demanding to know if there was anything she could do to help. But Trey's joy was short-lived. A quick glance in the rear-view mirror was enough to tell him that the driver of the car chasing them had been just as successful at evading the Packard *and was still right on their tail*!

Alex could not believe what had just happened. In the space of less than a minute he'd almost been involved in a head-on collision with another car, which, he had to admit, was a pretty scary moment. Then Davis had pulled off an extremely nifty and impressive piece of driving that had saved the day – the Packard missing the other car by half a gnat's whisker. Finally Davis had followed *that* by somehow managing not to hit the other two motors that it turned out were chasing after the first one at some speed. The chauffeur had now stopped the Packard, his face quite pale, and was gripping the steering wheel and breathing very, very deeply.

But these were by no means the most extraordinary things that had occurred. Top of *that* list was the fact that the first car had, unless he was a monkey's uncle, been driven by Trey! He was one hundred per cent sure of it. Added to which, he definitely recognized the driver of the second car as one of Mario's men, who had had Tony Burrell and a couple of the other guys with him; he hadn't the first idea who was in the third.

The big questions were, of course:

1. Why was Tony Burrell chasing Trey when he was supposed to be finding out if he'd been kidnapped or not?

2. Whose car was Trey driving? And,

3. Where the heck had he learned to drive like that?

"Hey, Ma, didja see that?" In the silence, Alex leaped up and looked round. "Ain't Davis the bee's knees, Ma? Ma, you okay?"

Alex's mother, along with Guido's wife and daughter, Arianna, had been completely unaware that anything was up until right at the very last minute – Davis, the chauffeur, not wanting to alarm them. Which was why Alex's mother had been applying some lipstick when the car had gone careering half off the road, and then back onto it again. She now sported a bright red slash of colour from lip to left ear, which made her look like she had a strangely ghoulish smile.

"Okay? Do I *look* like I should be okay, Alex? Davis, what in *heaven's* name happened back there?"

Mrs. Vittrano and Arianna, who had so far not said a word, both looked at Alex's mother and burst into tears simultaneously. Alex couldn't tell if this was because of the lipstick or the driving, but thought it best not to enquire.

"I must apologize, ma'am." Davis blinked and did a tiny shiver, which had nothing at all to do with him being cold. "There was almost a terrible accident... someone driving down the road straight at us, ma'am."

"*At* us?" Alex's mother stopped trying to repair the damage to her make-up. "Why *us*?"

The possibility that there had been an attempt on their lives only made Arianna and Mrs. Vittrano cry even more and even louder.

"No, Ma, it was someone being chased by Tony – Mr. Burrell." For some reason, he didn't know why, Alex thought that now was probably not the best time to announce that the driver of the car that had so very nearly crashed into them was his new friend from school.

"What's Mr. Burrell doing *chasing* people, for crying out loud?" Alex's mother looked back at the mirror in her powder compact. "Davis, get back to the house, before someone else tries to turn us all into strawberry jello!"

"Did you see who that was?" Tony Burrell looked over his shoulder at the fast disappearing rear of the two-tone Packard.

The driver nodded. "I did."

"Jeez…" Tony whistled. "That was *close*."

"You're telling me, boss."

"And what about the guy we now have on *our* tail?"

"You think he's a cop?" The driver glanced in his wing mirror.

"Can't be too careful." Tony looked over his shoulder at one of the men in the back. "You brought your typewriter with you?"

"Never go anywhere without it, Tony." The man patted the polished wooden stock of the Thompson sub-machine gun, next to him on the seat, along with a couple of extra 50-round drum magazines.

"Keep it ready, you never know when we might need it." Tony Burrell squared his shoulders. "Time we quit fooling around…let's get that car stopped!"

29 THE QUIET IS SHATTERED

The phone call to the Bureau's Chicago office had been picked up immediately, and the message passed on, with the utmost speed, to the relevant person. This person being Captain Robert B. Maynard, who had been waiting at the Country Inn for the return of his two men in the Ford saloon.

Now Captain Maynard and his men were primed for action – their two cars, one on either side of the blacktop, were each parked at a forty-five degree angle and waiting to be driven out to block the road. They were all set and eager to go, guns at the ready but still kept holstered and out of sight. If the new recruit, McKelldry, had it right and Tony Burrell was up here and up to something, it might give them the excuse they needed to take a good look at what was going on at Twelve Oaks. On the other hand, if he was wrong then everyone knew McKelldry's chances of staying in the new squad were non-existent.

Then, round a bend in the road, they saw a car matching the description McKelldry had given, and behind it the one he'd said was doing the chasing. Everyone moved into position, with Captain Maynard standing up on the running board of one of the cars to check out what he could see with his army-issue binoculars.

"Blow me down..." Captain Maynard took the binoculars away from his eyes, frowning.

"Sir?" queried the man nearest to him.

"There *is* a kid driving!"

"How we gonna handle this one, sir?"

"Start the cars and move 'em as *soon* as he's through." Captain Maynard jumped off the running board. "McKelldry's got the rear position covered, so Burrell's got nowhere to go."

"Think he'll make a fight of it, sir?"

"Listen up, everyone – do *not* fire until and unless *they* do, understood?"

"Yes *sir!*" came the response.

Two men got into their vehicles and cranked up the engines, the remaining two officers waiting in the lee of the cars, which they would use to fire from behind, if they had reason to do so. It was fairly obvious to everyone present that, if this didn't go pretty much like clockwork, things could get messy. Then they saw Captain Maynard walk out and stand right in the middle of the road...

Trey was just beginning to think he couldn't take many more surprises when he saw the two cars parked on either side of the road. Surely they couldn't be waiting for them...could they? And if they were, *how* had the people behind him managed to organize that?

There was no time to think of anything clever to do, and anyway, nowhere else to go but straight ahead. Trey was ready for all this to stop. He'd had it *up to here* with being chased and having no way of escaping. Trent Gripp *always* managed to snatch some kind of victory right out of the jaws of whatever disastrous situation he found himself in. Always. And although he knew very well that Trent Gripp was a made-up person, in the back of his mind Trey wanted to believe that in real life there would also, somehow, always be a way out. Which was when he saw the man walk from behind one of the cars and stand in the middle of the road. He was beckoning with his right hand and holding up something shiny in his left.

"You credit that, boy?" Shady shook his head in disbelief. "Looks like we be pulled over for speeding! Must be a *angel* on our shoulder, as when in this life is there *ever* po-leece when you really need 'em? You tell me that!"

Tony Burrell's driver took his foot off the accelerator slightly, letting the distance increase between them and the car in front. "Boss?"

"I got a bad feeling about this..." Tony glanced over his shoulder at the car behind them, then stared straight ahead. "Looks like they're going to let those guys through and have *us* in a bind...I'd say we've been set up good and proper. Hung out to dry."

"Who'd do a thing...?"

"Who knew where we were? Who knew?"

"Mario? He wouldn't..."

"Not *Mario*, you idiot! Had to be that rat Bowyer Dunne! He knew he was in big trouble and must've made some kind of a deal." Tony reached into his jacket and pulled out his chromed Colt automatic. "We gotta get back to the house...don't let me down!"

The driver, whose nickname was "The Wheel", did not need to be told twice.

Captain Maynard stepped back, his overcoat tails swinging like the toreador's cape in a movie about bullfighters he'd once seen; as the Chrysler 50 flew past him, the face of the kid driving a grimace of concentration and fear, Captain Maynard let the car on his right move in front of him across the road. The next few seconds were going to be crucial. Would the pursuing car stop or fight?

In the event, it did neither.

Somehow – and later everyone would agree that if they hadn't seen it with their own eyes, they wouldn't have believed it – the driver of the dark red Pontiac pulled off what could only be described as a pretty darned astonishing move. One moment the car was coming straight at the roadblock, and the next the rear end had spun round like the car was a toy on a spindle; in a space that looked far too narrow, and in a matter of yards, it was facing the opposite direction! Tyres squealed like stuck pigs, exhaust smoke billowed and grit flew every which way as the car came to a momentary halt, rocking on its suspension. Then, engine roaring, it took off the way it had come. Straight for the Bureau vehicle coming down the road.

This was so unexpected that for a split second Captain Maynard was at a loss as to what to do next. That moment's hesitation was all it took to let all hell break loose.

Instead of getting out of the way of the oncoming car, the Ford saloon kept going right for it, a decision which caused two men to appear from the rear windows of the Pontiac, guns blazing.

Refusing to take the hail of bullets as a hint, the driver of the Ford put it into a skid that just clipped the front offside wing of the Pontiac as the driver tried to avoid him. The collision sent the Ford tumbling over on its side and fractured its gas tank, which proceeded to ignite when gasoline spilled onto the intensely hot exhaust system; and then the tank exploded. This happened just after the driver had managed to exit through the smashed front windscreen.

Apart from damaging a very fine paint job, the Ford's impact burst one of the Pontiac's front tyres and broke both the tie rods. This brought the Pontiac to an abrupt, lurching halt and caused the four occupants to be thrown forwards with some force. The gunman still hanging out of the rear window carried on like a stone from a catapult when the car stopped. He landed awkwardly more than fifteen feet down the road, ending up with a broken clavicle and scapula, a shattered right humerus, plus a punctured lung, some serious cuts and grazes and a mild concussion. His colleagues came out of the Pontiac dazed but, despite that, with guns blazing.

All this happened in far less time than it took to tell the story the next day in the squad room.

As the scene unfolded Captain Maynard sent one man back to check on the folks in the Chrysler, then yelled "Fire at will!", even though he was no longer in the army. As his men – apart from the driver of the Ford saloon – hadn't been thrown around in an auto accident, their shooting was much more accurate than the fierce, but unfocused gunfire they were up against.

Chunks of hot lead whistled through the air, thudded into the steel bodywork of the cars blocking the road, and ploughed through the tempered glass of at least one windshield. The noise was deafening. And then Captain Maynard saw someone come into his line of sight with a sub-machine gun, tossing slugs here, there and everywhere else. The Captain was about to try and get a shot off when he saw the man twist sideways, his hat flying off as a couple of bullets ripped into his upper torso. A quick glance showed he'd been shot by the new boy, McKelldry, who'd been driving the crashed saloon. He had blood streaming down his face from a cut scalp, and was kneeling in a two-handed pose that was straight out of the textbooks.

Silence fell, broken only by the noisy crackle of the Ford burning up.

A shiny, chromed automatic pistol arced up from somewhere behind the dark red Pontiac, and landed with a dull clunk on the blacktop; it was followed by a second pistol and then a hand appeared waving what looked like a monogrammed white handkerchief.

"Don't shoot!" Tony Burrell yelled, standing up, hands empty and raised. "I'm done!"

"Me too, okay?" A second figure stood up next to Tony Burrell, his nose bloody and bruised from where he'd hit it on the steering wheel. "Me too..."

30 AFTERMATH

Thinking that now they'd be safe and everything was going to be just fine, Trey sped through the gap between what he hoped with all his might really were two police cars. Screeching to a halt, he was so relieved he got the pedals all mixed up and stalled the car.

"Sorry..." Trey felt quite shaky, and his arms ached. "You know, if I scared anyone."

"You got nothing to apologize for, kid." Mr. Pisbo grunted with pain. "Nothing at all."

"Well I for one – being as how *I* had a ringside seat, Pisbo – beg to differ!"

"Cut it out, Shady..."

Trey was about to reach for the ignition to start it again when he realized that he didn't have to worry about flooding the carburettor or any of that stuff. Instead, he hauled up the parking brake and allowed himself to ease up a bit, slumping back in his seat. And no sooner had he done so than it seemed like the Gunfight at the OK Corral had broken out all over again behind him.

"I am starting to take this real *personal*, Pisbo!"

"I said cut it *out*, Shady..."

Before this discussion could go any further, there was a man at Trey's window, somewhat curtly making it clear that they should all stay where they were for the moment...and the next minute the same person was dashing away saying they should get the heck down and not move. Which, considering the sudden outbreak of shooting, Trey thought seemed like extremely good advice well worth taking. Even without Mr. Pisbo yelling *"HIT-THE-FLOOR!"* at the top of his voice from the back of the car.

Tucked down under the steering wheel, the sound of bullets whistling by outside the car, Trey was astonished to see Shady still sitting on the seat next to him, nonchalantly tamping a cigarette on his thumbnail.

"Shady…" Trey tugged at Shady's trouser leg. "Mr. Jones…there's *shooting* out there, you going to get down out of the way?"

"I figure, I was cat, I'd have by rights done with *at least* four of my lives today." Shady got ready to strike a match. "So, seeing as how I *ain't* no cat, my time surely must be up by now. And there ain't *no point* hiding from the Reaper when he come to get you, boy, no point at all."

"*Shady…!*"

Whatever Mr. Pisbo was yelling at Shady was drowned out by the vicious tap dance of a machine gun opening up, followed by one of the Chrysler's headlamps exploding as a stray bullet found a home. Trey, curled up tighter than a dog on a cold night, was astonished to see, out of the corner of his eye, Shady calmly light his cigarette and blow the match out.

It occurred to him that *he* could've been relaxing like that…safely at home, sitting at his desk with a glass of malted milk and a couple of cookies, doing his homework. Then it occurred to him that this might very well be it, the Big Goodbye, as Trent Gripp often referred to dying. He kind of hoped not. Although, if it was, at least he'd seen Alex (who didn't look the least bit kidnapped) sitting in the front seat of the car he'd so very nearly crashed into. A small comfort, as his gramps would say.

It was as Trey was wondering if his parents would be proud of him, or just mad *at* him, for being killed in a shoot-out between some no-good hoodlums and the police that he realized it had gone quiet. No more shooting.

Trey poked his head above the car seat. "Can we get up now, Mr. Pisbo?"

"What do *he* know, hugging the floor carpet back there?" Shady wound down his window and stuck his head out. "My oh my, surely look like they's been a outbreak of no little civil unrest back there!"

"Is it safe?"

"Heck, boy," Shady glanced down at Trey, still huddled underneath the steering wheel, "cain't see how *you* be scared a *nuthin'* after the drive you all just gave us!"

Trey got himself up onto the seat as Velma and a waxy-pale Mr. Pisbo came into view, Mr. Pisbo looking, it had to be said, a little the worse for wear and tear. Between them, Banjo the Boston terrier appeared like a jack-in-the-box to joyously lick both their faces. Here was a pooch, Trey thought, that knew it was lucky to be alive.

Winding his own window down, Trey leaned out and looked back the way they'd come. There was a sharp, acrid smell in the air, coming no doubt from the overturned car that was on fire on the other side of the roadblock. And he could also see the red auto that had been chasing them, oddly enough, facing the wrong way *up* the road, its front fender all buckled. Which was not to mention the fact that it was peppered with bullet holes. Two men stood quite near the crashed red car, their hands in the air; one had a bloody nose, and the other looked unhurt and somehow quite familiar, though Trey couldn't imagine how that might be.

"Trey, quick! I think my dad needs help..."

"Help? Right!" Pressing the handle down, Trey elbowed the door open; Mr. Pisbo was in trouble, and whichever way you looked at it, *he* was kind of responsible. "I'll be right back!"

The private detective character – with a bullet wound in his leg he was being less than forthcoming about – had really begun to annoy Captain Maynard. So far the shamus was not saying very much, stating client privilege – the client being the kid – which was now very high on Captain Maynard's personal list of lame excuses. He'd been about to get the man's daughter out of the room, so he could lay some of his own personal law down on him, when the Bureau Chief, Mr. Bonner, had called.

Always right there, always up to speed, Chief Bonner had been informed about the message to the emergency line, and the request for a roadblock, and he wanted to know what the outcome of the operation was; Fox Lake, he'd reminded Captain Maynard, was not a place used to police activities such as these.

Captain Maynard, who prided himself on doing everything by the book, had told his boss exactly what had occurred, giving him a bullet-by-bullet account of events. He'd made a special mention of the fact that a kid had been driving one of the cars – after all, that kind of thing did not happen every day of the week – and then he'd listed everyone who'd been involved. Chief Bonner had stopped him when he'd read out the kid's name, demanding that he repeat what he'd just said, and then that he "go and check for dang sure" he had the name right. Because, if he had, the boy was the grandson of one of Mr. Bonner's oldest and closest associates.

The Captain, who did not believe in coincidences, wondered what the chances were that there was something going on he didn't know about. Because it made you think, when the grandson of a close associate of the Bureau Chief turned up being chased by one of Mario Andrusa's fixers. It really did.

Leaving the Country Inn, to "go and check for dang sure" what the boy's name was, Captain Maynard stopped and surveyed the scene down the road. Devastation was probably too extreme a word to use, but only just. And the fact that only one person had died was as close to miraculous as he'd ever got in his professional career with the Chicago police force, given the amount of lead there'd been flung. Destruction of property was another thing altogether. They were *not* going to be happy about the state of the Ford back at the office...

Trey sat on the Chrysler's running board, next to Shady Jones, where they'd both been told to stay; Banjo was lying, disconsolate, at his feet. Mr. Pisbo was in the nearby Country Inn, along with Velma, where a local doctor was looking after him, as well as a wounded cop and one of the gangsters who'd gotten himself all busted up in the shoot-out.

And on the other side of the cars, which had been used as a roadblock, there was a dead man, covered in a piece of tarpaulin. Trey had seen the body before they'd put the tarp over it.

"They're not going to arrest us, are they, Shady?"

"*Us?* Only one person driving that car, boy, and it weren't me. Or even the darn dog."

Coming towards them, Trey could see the man he'd

worked out was in charge; he'd heard the other cops call him "Cap" and had gathered his name was Maynard. The man had a real serious expression on his face, and all thoughts of his own imminent arrest evaporated as Trey thought maybe he was coming with bad news about Mr. Pisbo. Banjo obviously must've had similar notions as he retreated between Trey's legs, growling.

"Okay, son." Captain Maynard stopped a few feet in front of Trey and Shady, taking out a notebook and the chewed stub of a pencil. "What did you say your name was?"

"Me?" Trey pointed to himself.

"You."

"Why, what'd I do, sir?"

"Nothing, I just need to check your name."

"Hope you gots a good lawyer, boy…"

Trey shot Shady a heartfelt glower. "MacIntyre," he said, stroking Banjo's head, tickling him behind his ear. It calmed them both down.

"Full name, son." Captain Maynard licked his pencil, waiting.

"T. Drummond MacIntyre…the third."

"And the T…?"

"Theodore, the T. stands for Theodore."

"They's two *more* of you Theodores?" Shady looked Trey up and down in mock amazement.

"You wouldn't, by any chance, be related to Ace MacIntyre, would you?"

"Yeah." Trey nodded. "He's my gramps...my grandfather, why?"

"Just checking I'd been given the correct information..." Captain Maynard finished making a note, turned on his heel and began walking away. "Stay put, both of you."

"Hey, but what about Mr. Pisbo?" Trey stood up. "How is he?"

"He'll live."

Trey sat down with a thump, the Chrysler's suspension squeaking; he watched the Captain go back into the Country Inn, which they now seemed to be using as a temporary HQ as it had a phone. "Why didn't he ask you for your name, Shady?"

"Either he know *all* about me, or he don't care a jot *who* I am." Shady took a little sip from his hip flask. "Not sure which I like least."

"Right." Captain Maynard, now in his shirtsleeves, put down his coffee cup and looked round the barroom at his men. McKelldry was there, a plaster on his forehead, his face pretty much cleaned up, as was the officer he'd dropped off to make the phone call to the Chicago office.

"We have one more job to do to wrap this whole thing up and get on our way. Because Tony Burrell has given us the excuse we needed to make a visit to Twelve Oaks, right on a plate."

One of the men shifted in his chair, leaning it back on two legs. "We have a warrant, boss?"

Captain Maynard nodded. "Chief Bonner has a local judge issuing one as we speak. Be here any time now."

"And when we get there?" the man inquired.

"We turn the place over, good and proper."

"Mr. Andrusa's not gonna like that, boss. And *we* are no doubt gonna catch some mud for busting in there, warrant or no warrant, the people he has in his pocket."

"The whole point of this squad," Captain Maynard looked at each of his men in turn, "is that we're above the backhanders and back room deals...*we* are in no one's pocket."

"What's gonna happen to the prisoners, and the, ah, *not* prisoners, Cap?" A man standing by the bar poured some sugar into his coffee mug.

"They will all stay here, until reinforcements arrive from Chicago; then they get to go home or go to jail. Or the morgue." Captain Maynard nodded at McKelldry. "And you get to stay here, finish off taking statements and make sure the right people go to the right places, Officer."

"But boss!"

"No buts…you did real good today, but the doc said to make sure you took it easy for a bit…sorry. Orders." Captain Maynard took his automatic out of his shoulder holster, released its magazine and checked the load. "And the rest of you, we move out in *five* minutes!"

31 TIME TO GO

Davis cornered fast off the road and accelerated up the driveway, pebbles and small stones shooting up from the rear wheels like grapeshot. The drive back to the house had been something of a test of endurance, what with Mrs. Vittrano and her daughter wailing like banshees, and Mrs. Klein, trying to make herself heard above the racket, insisting he go faster. All that after the near collision. It made him wonder if it wasn't time to look for a new job.

Slowing down as he approached the house, Davis

had hardly brought the Packard to a halt than the women were out the back of the car and running up the front steps like someone had opened a box of spiders. Beside him he could see the boy, Alex, shaking his head as he opened his door.

"You okay, Alex?" Davis switched the engine off.

"Me? I'm *fine*, Davis." Alex stopped halfway through getting out of the car. "Don't you sometimes wish my dad had bought a model with one of those glass panels behind the driver that you can slide closed? Something to keep the noise out? I know I do."

"They got scared."

Alex stopped closing the door. "Imagine what they'd have been like if there really *had* been an accident – you think we should get in there and explain what happened?"

"I suppose we better had..." Davis looked at Alex. "By the way, did you see who was driving the other car – the one that didn't quite hit us?"

"The boy?"

Davis let out a sigh of relief. "Am *I* glad you said that."

"Why?"

"Thought I'd imagined it, is why..."

"Want to know something weird, Davis?"

"What could be weirder than some kid driving a car that was being chased by Mr. Burrell?"

"We know him, you and me..."

* * *

"I'm not kidding, Dad, honest!"

Alex was back in the room where Uncle Mario had quizzed him the night before. He was with Davis, and this time it was just his father asking the questions. Someone had opened the windows to air the place out, but the stale aroma of cigars, whiskey and aftershave still hung around; Alex reckoned, no matter what you did, it would always be there, soaked into everything.

Nate Klein chewed his lip as his glance flicked between his son and his chauffeur. "You both saw this, right?" Davis and Alex nodded. "You're telling me the getaway car Tony was chasing was being driven by your *friend*, Alex?"

"What I said, Dad." Alex shrugged and readjusted his glasses. "If I was going to make something up, it would be a whole lot better story than that, believe me."

"Sure, sure..." Nate Klein paced up and down, rubbing his chin, lost in thought. If the boy they thought might've been kidnapped by Dunne's man, Joe Cullen, was driving the car, then surely it *couldn't* be Cullen who'd been watching the house; but, if it wasn't him, who was it? Then he came to an abrupt halt. "This is not good, this is *not* good. Davis, I want you to get the motor ready; Alex, go pack your things *now*! We are leaving!"

* * *

After a visit to the housekeeper, telling her to shift up a gear and get the staff to start packing everyone's bags, Nate Klein dashed back to the room where Mario was still harassing Bowyer Dunne. He didn't bother to knock.

"Mario, I think something's up!"

"Oh yeah?" Mario, who had been bending over a cowed Bowyer Dunne, stood up. "I heard a hullabaloo fit to wake the dead when the ladies came back. What weren't they happy about...champagne not cold enough for them?"

"Something's screwy...I need to talk to you, outside." Nate walked past Mario and opened the French windows onto the patio; Mario came out after him, a dubious expression on his face.

"What's this about, Nate?"

"I got a bad feeling and it's giving me stomach gyp. Whoever it was back up there," he pointed at where the intruder had first been spotted, "for sure he wasn't Dunne's man, Cullen, come to help him."

"He wasn't? Then..."

"This isn't going to make *any* kind of sense, but whoever he is, he was with the kid, MacIntyre's grandson. The one we thought Cullen was after. Alex saw him, in the car they must've come here in, being chased by Tony." Nate made a whatever-next face. "Alex swears blind the kid was driving, but be that as it may, I do not like unexplained things happening around us, it makes me nervous. I think we should go, and we should go now. In fact, forgive me if you disagree, Mario, but I have already put things in motion to do such."

"You mean *run*?" Mario's eyes saucered. "Mario Andrusa doesn't run from anybody, Nate, you should know that!"

"Mario, Mario..." Nate made calm-down motions with his hands. "This isn't about running, this is about not *being* here, in this house, if – more likely *when* – we get visitors. Let's get back to Chicago, where we know what's what and who's who...any case, it's too open out here, far too many people we don't know and who don't owe us for my liking."

"What about Dunne?" Mario nodded back at the house.

"I was thinking about that, and I had an idea: we leave him here."

"*Leave* him? I haven't finished with the bozo yet!"

"Let whoever turns up here, be it the cops or whoever, let *them* deal with him, Mario. Let *Dunne* explain what he's doing here all on his ownsome. I'm sure he'll be very convincing, as the *last* thing he wants is to talk about how well he knows us."

"What's to stop him from high-tailing it the moment we're gone?"

"Fear, Mario. Fear that you'll find out he did and come after him..."

Bowyer Dunne was getting drunk. And feeling increasingly sorry for himself. Becoming Republican party treasurer, Mid-West, had been the pinnacle, the very acme and zenith of his political career so far. And now it looked like he was in a defective elevator, headed south and directly for rock-bottom. He poured himself another couple or more fingers of Mario Andrusa's outstanding Scotch. I mean, why not? The man had left him in charge of the house.

Cursing the day he'd *ever* crossed the path of that Sicilian snake-in-the-grass, Bowyer weaved his way across the room, only spilling a drop or two of the pale yellow liquid as he sat down heavily in one of the leather armchairs. Mind you, he reminded himself, he really had no one else to blame for his present predicament – it had all been his very own clever-clever idea to get involved with Mario and his people.

On the face of it, it had been a *great* idea! At the time, he'd thought it was one of his best, because both sides wanted the self-same thing: to win the election; to elect Herbert Hoover and to keep the country Republican for at *least* another four years. And with the money Mario had at his disposal, there'd been plenty of ways to see that the Democratic candidate, Al Smith, wouldn't have a chance – from Minnesota to Texas and Illinois to Kansas – come November.

With Hoover in the White House, everyone got what they wanted: Bowyer moved up the ladder in the Republican party, and Mario got the continuation of Prohibition for as long as possible. It being as good as a licence to print money. With that kind of situation at stake, early on there'd even been talk – if Smith had looked like having a real chance – of some kind of accident to remove him permanently from the picture.

The word "assassination" was never explicitly used, but Bowyer remembered being shocked, and also excited, that the notion was being seriously discussed by men he knew personally. Looking back, that was when he should've realized he was way out of his depth; that it might not be such a good idea to be doing business with types who didn't give a second thought to doing such things as "getting rid" of a Presidential candidate. Even if he was a Catholic.

But Bowyer hadn't thought that. Instead, he'd enjoyed being pals with men who really did light their cigars with $100 bills, who literally had money to burn. These were men who, as long as things were going their way, could be very generous indeed; although, as he was

274

discovering, when things *didn't* go their way...

Bowyer tried hard to change that particular train of thought, but the only other thing that came to mind was the part old man MacIntyre *had* to have played in what he was now thinking of as his downfall. And, once again, Bowyer saw the finger of blame pointing directly at himself...if *he* hadn't got it into his head that he was going to somehow push and shove MacIntyre into selling him the Circle M ranch, well it stood to reason that MacIntyre would never have sent that darn picture-taking grandson of his to spy on him! And *he* wouldn't be sitting here now, up to his neck in more muck and manure than you could shake a stick at.

Knocking back the whiskey in one go, its soft, anaesthetic glow curling down his gullet, Bowyer became aware that there was someone standing in the open doorway. And they didn't look like a member of the estate's staff...something about the gun in their hand, and the trilby and grey-brown overcoat they were wearing, being the clues there.

"Who you?" Bowyer screwed up his eyes, trying to focus better. "Everyone's gone...no one here, 'cept little ole me..."

"Someone's at home, Cap!" the man called out as he came across the room. "What's your name, sir?"

"Bowyer." Bowyer stared at his whiskey tumbler.

"Empty…" he said, and botched an attempt at standing up.

"Mr. Bowyer…"

"Nope!" Bowyer waggled a finger and shook his head at the man now standing a few feet away from him. "*Not* Mist Bowyer…Mist *Dunne!*"

"Okay, Mr. Dunne, what are you doing here…where is everybody?"

"Dunno." Bowyer made an almighty effort to get up, launching himself to his feet; delighted, and not a little surprised to find that he'd made it, he stood, swaying like some ungainly plant in a stiff wind for a couple of seconds. But this endeavour had taken it out of him. On top of which, his nerves were shot, he hadn't eaten anything since he couldn't remember when – but he *had* drunk really quite a lot of Scotch – and the combination was lethal. Bowyer blacked out.

The Bureau officer watched as the man in front of him dropped the heavy cut-glass tumbler he was holding and then fell to the ground, face first, like he'd been chopped down. He hit the carpet with a thud and didn't move. The officer approached, kneeled down and felt the man's neck for a pulse; he wasn't dead, but the officer suspected, from the smell, that he was dead drunk.

"You have to whack him?"

The officer looked back over his shoulder to see Captain Maynard coming into the room. "I didn't hit him, Cap, *he* hit the bottle – three sheets to wind, and then some, I'd say." Standing up, he pointed at the whiskey glass.

"Who is he?"

"Says his name's Dunne, leastways that's what I *think* he was trying to tell me."

"Bowyer Dunne, by any chance?"

"Spot on, Cap; how'd you know?"

"Chief Bonner has mentioned him as a 'person of interest', but I was under the impression he was down in Topeka."

"Anyone else here?'

Captain Maynard shook his head. "The birds have flown, no doubt back to their swanky nests in Chicago. Which makes me wonder, who tipped them off we were coming?"

"You think we got a leak in the squad, Cap?"

"I think it has to be a possibility..."

32 AT THE END OF THE DAY

Trey looked at his watch as the unmarked police saloon car turned into his street. Twenty to seven, and still light. He'd promised Mrs. Cooke he'd be home in time for an early supper, and with just minutes to spare. Only he hadn't reckoned on being escorted upstairs by a plain-clothes police officer, who he knew had specific instructions to deliver him to the door of his apartment and see him safely inside.

He was on his own now as Mr. Shady Jones, who had told Trey he was not at all keen to spend any more of his time around po-leece than he *absolutely* had to, had asked to be dropped at the first train station they came to. And another police officer was driving Mr. Pisbo and Velma, along with Banjo, home in the Chrysler which, apart from the shot-up headlight, had survived the day pretty much intact. A fact that had made Mr. Pisbo swear he'd never buy any other make of automobile.

What the exact and final outcome of the shoot-out had been, Trey wasn't entirely sure, because, as per usual, no one would tell him a single thing. All he did know was that Captain Maynard had left with a bunch of men "to see what was up at the Twelve Oaks place". On the plus side, he had at least remembered where he'd seen the man before, the one who'd emerged unscathed from the car that had been chasing them. It was Tony Burrell, the person he'd photographed posing by the Duesenberg at the T-Bone ranch party – and who was still waiting for the picture he'd paid so handsomely for! It had to be some kind of coincidence; even though Austin J. Randall was pretty clear that he did not believe in coincidences, and neither should anyone wanting to be a Private Investigator.

As the car approached the Tavistock Building, Trey could see that work had started on the repairs to the foyer, with at least one of the broken mirrors already replaced. He wondered if the foyer's marble floor was still blood-stained.

It was only last night – not even twenty-four hours ago, he reminded himself – when the elevator doors had opened and he'd been presented with the aftermath of the shooting: the body on the floor, the smell of cordite, the blood, the men with pistols, a whole extraordinary picture made up of things he'd only ever imagined before. He remembered how he'd fallen asleep dreaming of some cops'n'robbers scene from a movie, with a car being chased up the street as a hoodlum sprayed the vicinity with his tommy gun. And here he was, coming home after having been involved in just such a "type of incident". Only *he'd* been in the driving seat.

"You all right, son?" The policeman pulled up by the Tavistock. "You look a tad thoughtful."

"Just thinking about today…I, um, I coulda got killed…"

"From what I hear, you are one lucky kid – that was some set-to you got yourself involved in there. Is it true what they told me, that you were driving one of the cars?" Trey nodded, and the officer cut the engine. "Bet *that* wasn't what you had in mind when you left here this morning."

Trey got out of the car. "Sure wasn't, mister…"

He'd left the building hoping to discover what had

happened to Alex, only to find himself right in the middle of the kind of action he'd read about in *Black Ace* magazine any number of times but never, *ever* thought he would actually be caught up in. Oddest of all, in the midst of all the hair-raising activity – the rescue, the shooting, the near-miss and the general panic of the chase – he *had* seen Alex! In that moment, as the Chrysler and the two-tone Packard rocketed past each other, a hair's breadth apart, their eyes had locked in a mixture of stunned recognition and utter amazement.

Then, in the little time Mr. Pisbo had had before being taken off to be looked at by a doctor, he'd told Trey, Velma and Shady to all keep their lips firmly buttoned about the *real* reason why they were out in Fox Lake. They should, he'd said, just claim they'd come out for a picnic, with Trey coming along to keep Velma company. If questioned, they were to have no idea why they'd been shot at and chased. Shady had said that was fine by him, as he rarely had *any* idea what Mr. Pisbo was up to, and Mr. Pisbo had replied that everything was also fine by *him*, as Shady wouldn't have to try very hard to act dumb.

The long and the short of it, Trey thought as he and the policeman crossed the foyer and made for the elevators, was that he hadn't said anything to anyone, particularly about having seen Alex. Not even to Mr.

Pisbo. But the fact was, he'd seen Alex out at Fox Lake, sitting up front with his chauffeur, Davis. Which either meant he'd somehow managed to escape his kidnappers, or had never been kidnapped in the first place...and if that was the case, what *had* Trey seen happen through his binoculars down on the street?

And then there he was, standing outside the front door of his apartment, the policeman rapping on it with his knuckles. Trey took a deep breath and tried to prepare himself for what was, no doubt about it, going to be an evening of being royally told off. While this would not be a first for him, he had a feeling it might well be an occasion to remember. When the door opened and he found himself looking at Mrs. Cooke and not his mother or father, Trey felt that maybe his luck had changed. If only a little.

"As good as your word, Mr. Trey, as good as your word; your father's home, so get yourself ready for dinner, lickety-split now!" Mrs. Cooke beamed at Trey and then looked askance at the officer standing next to him. "I think that will be all, young man."

The officer, who was about to say something when the door was summarily shut in his face, decided that life was too short and he'd rather get back to his station house, sign off and get home. It was, after all, Saturday night.

33 QUID PRO QUO

For the first time, Trey thought probably in his entire life, he had positively *welcomed* a Monday morning during term time. It had been a tad trying, at home. For everyone.

To begin with, everything had seemed pretty much okay as his parents appeared not to have been informed about *The Fox Lake Incident*. Instead, his father's attentions had been solely focused on Friday night's break-in, and the shooting downstairs. The arrival of a couple of police officers to interview Trey about it hadn't done much to keep him out of the spotlight, and he did come in for some stick for leaving the apartment armed with a baseball bat, but it had all come down to a mild enough telling off for "inappropriate behaviour".

In Trey's opinion there really hadn't been the need, right there and then, to complicate matters by going into detail about what had happened out at Fox Lake. After all, he was fine; amazingly enough, considering what had occurred, there was not a scratch on him. And there had been a point where he'd wondered if it would *ever* be necessary to come clean, which he should've *known* was wishful thinking on his part. The situation deteriorated somewhat once the cops had left – and after his father had taken a phone call from Gramps. Then he really had got it in the neck.

There'd been a niggling concern at the back of Trey's mind ever since Captain Maynard had asked him if he was related to Ace MacIntyre. He could not for the life of him work out why he'd wanted to know that, *or* what gramps could possibly have to do with anything. Well, so much for Austin J. Randall not believing in coincidences, was all he had to say about the matter! What with his gramps and Captain Maynard's boss going way back and being the best of pals.

Which was how it had *all* come out. Every last detail.

The end result of his father's exhaustive and stern inquisition had been that Trey was sent to bed early and grounded for a month. A month! For being something of a hero! Leastways, that was how *he* saw it. And he wasn't the only one to get it. His father had made it quite clear that he held his mom *and* Mrs. Cooke responsible for letting Trey "run riot" while he was away.

As he walked through the Mount Vernon Academy gates that chill September morning, the only shine Trey could put on the whole deal at home was that at least his father did not hold with corporal punishment. Striding up the main path he kept his eyes peeled for Alex. He could hardly wait to get the low-down on what had happened.

That day, like every other Monday, Trey's timetable meant that he would not be in the same class as Alex all day. He should, though, run into him at a break, or at lunch; that was how he'd originally engineered meeting him. But Alex was nowhere to be found.

Searching out someone he knew was in the same home room as Alex, Trey heard the rumour doing the rounds that Alex had left and was going back to New York. His first thought was that he hadn't had the chance to say goodbye, and the second that it was a shame they'd never get to know each other better, because he had a feeling that, under different circumstances, they might have been firm friends. But, if your dad was connected with the Mob, being friends was always going to be difficult.

After school, walking home on his own and trying to figure out how to convince his dad to change his mind about grounding him for so long, Trey got the distinct feeling he was being watched. The previous night, having had his lights turned out early, he had flattened his torch batteries by reading some more of *How to Become a Private Eye in 10 Easy Lessons* under the covers. In the chapter entitled *Learning to Trust Your Instincts*, Austin J. Randall had said that honing the ability to know when you were being watched was imperative. He'd been far too tired to get his dictionary and look up "honing" and "imperative", but he got the general gist.

Trey was fully aware that the one thing you should *never* do was let the person following you know that you knew you were being followed. But it was real hard not to look around, searching for the telltale signs – people studiously *not* looking at you was a big one – or taking evasive action. The whole way home the hairs on the back of Trey's neck were up and he felt like he had a target pinned on his back.

He tried to see if the same car kept on going past him, as that would've been a real giveaway, but he didn't want to be spotted staring at number plates. He also tried to keep an eye out for anyone looking particularly shifty, but saw nothing at all suspicious. So he was, to say the least, astonished when, as he neared his building, he heard someone behind him call his name. Glancing back he was bowled over to see Alex coming up the street towards him, smiling like nothing had changed when they both knew it had.

"I saw what happened, after you left here – it looked like you'd been kidnapped, Alex! I didn't know *what* to do, but I *had* to try and find out if you were okay!" They were up in Trey's room, tucking into the freshly baked walnut cake Mrs. Cooke had given them.

"Me as well! But they didn't mean to snatch *me*, Trey, they made a big mistake, those two guys...they were after *you*!" Alex brushed some crumbs off his mouth. "Great cake, by the way...actually, it was some pictures you'd taken they were really after, which I have a pretty good idea are the ones with Uncle Mario in them."

"How'd you know?"

"Heard 'em talking, just before they let me go, and

when you weren't home when I called I figured they must've gone back and kidnapped *you*!"

"I called *your* place!" Trey could hardly believe what he was hearing. "The person I talked to gave me some flim-flam about you not being at home, like the cops had told them to keep quite about you being lifted! Wait a second, wait a second..." Cogs whirred in Trey's head. "Those two guys were after my *pictures*?"

"Kind of...what one of them said was it was the film they wanted."

"So *that's* it!" Trey hit the palm of his hand with his fist.

"What is?"

"We got burglarized Friday night! Some guy got in, and a cop got shot in the foyer." Trey prepared to take another bite of cake. "There was a *lot* of blood, let me tell you."

"You saw it?"

Trey, his mouth now full, nodded.

"Was the guy dead?"

"Dunno..." If he was, Trey thought, then he'd seen two dead bodies in two days. Amongst a whole lot else. "So, you going back to, um...to New York? That's what the talk is...you know, at school."

"Yeah. We're going back..." Alex shrugged. "My ma never liked it here so much."

"Oh, right." Trey nodded sagely, thinking, no wonder, after what had happened at Fox Lake.

"What the heck were you doing out at Fox Lake?"

Alex's question, out of the blue like that, made Trey think that he must have mind-reading abilities.

"Looking for you...we were looking for you."

"We?" Alex looked shocked. "You were with your *parents*?"

"No! And sorry for nearly crashing into you, but we were being chased."

"Davis was *real* impressed with your driving." Alex grinned. "He said you did good not to hit us."

"My gramps taught me this summer, on the ranch." Trey put his plate down on his desk. "You won't believe what happened next!"

"The thing of it is," Alex looked at his wristwatch, "I gotta go, my dad's waiting for me downstairs, and I only really came up to say goodbye."

"Sure, right...you'd better..."

"But the *real* thing of it is..." Alex began nervously pacing the room, then stopped. "Would you let *me* have the film those guys were after?"

Taken aback by the completely unexpected turn in the conversation, Trey didn't know what to say. Was this the real reason Alex had turned up? Not to say a final goodbye, but to act as a middleman. And it had to be for his "Uncle" Mario – who else?

"It's for my Uncle Mario," Alex said, answering Trey's unasked question, "but he didn't tell me why."

"Oh, right…" Trey knew he sounded a bit off, then a small voice reminded him of what Trent Gripp always said: you were stuck with your family, but at least you could choose your friends. No matter that Trey had kind of faked becoming pals in the first place, he liked Alex and realized he'd miss him.

"Okay…you can have it." Trey went to his desk and pulled open a drawer. "You want the prints we made, too?"

"How much…?"

"Nothing." Trey shook his head as he handed over a 10x8 inch Manila envelope; apart from the fact that Tony Burrell had already paid over the odds for a picture he never got, he really would feel guilty about taking money when there was a complete set of prints at Mr. Pisbo's office. That would be dishonest.

Nate Klein sat forward and pointed out of the car's darkened windows. "There he is, Mario."

"Took his time about it." Mario Andrusa didn't look up, continuing to clean his nails with a small penknife.

"All good things…" Nate watched his son walk

towards the Cadillac, which was parked a block or two away from the Tavistock, and prepared to open the door for him to get in. "He has an envelope."

"He's a good kid, Nate. A real good kid, you should be proud of him."

"I am…" Nate pushed the handle down. "I certainly am."

"Sorry I took so long, Dad." Alex climbed in and sat down in the space between his father and his Uncle Mario, holding up the envelope. "I got it."

Mario snapped the blade of his knife shut, then took the proffered envelope. "How much?"

"Nothing – I asked and he said he didn't want a cent."

"We could learn a lesson here, Mario."

"Which is?" Mario picked up a black leather attaché case, opened it and put the envelope inside.

"Sometimes, all you gotta do is ask nice."

34 LOOSE ENDS

About a week later – or, as he liked to think of it, only a quarter of the way through his grounding – Trey came back from school, Friday afternoon, to find there had been visitors. Gramps and Gramma Cecilia were back in town! His mother said they wouldn't be around for long and that they'd come by for coffee and a selection of Mrs. Cooke's legendary baked goods. He'd missed them by about half an hour. But, his mother said, his gramps had asked her to tell him he'd be coming by Saturday, midday.

Mrs. MacIntyre looked up from the magazine she was reading. "He said to make sure you were here."

"Very funny, I don't think," Trey humphed out of the room, "seeing as how I'm a *prisoner* in this apartment, and do not need reminding I can't go anywhere else."

"I thought your father was remarkably restrained," his mother called after him, "considering what you'd gotten up to, Trey."

"Well how comes," Trey called back, "*you* didn't get grounded for not knowing where I was?"

"That's one of the privileges of being a grown-up...we have a different set of rules."

Tramping upstairs to his room, Trey wondered exactly how long it would be before *he* would be allowed to play the game by those rules. Even though there was no getting round the fact that he was still a child, being treated like one *all* the time ticked him off no end; particularly as part of his punishment was a ban on making – or receiving – phone calls. This meant Trey had been unable to call Velma to see how Mr. Pisbo was, or find out any details at all about...well about *anything*. What had happened when the police raided Twelve Oaks? He didn't know. What did the mobsters think Mr. Pisbo had seen to make them so keen on getting their hands on him? He did not know. Questions he *could've* asked Alex when he came round, but hadn't had the time. And now Alex was back in New York.

Sometimes life, in his considered opinion, was extremely unfair...

It being a Saturday, normally Trey would have had plans. But not today. Today his options were really quite limited, but at least there was one avenue of escape still open to him. He had, for the last forty minutes or so, been thoroughly immersed in a gripping story called "The Darker Side of Sunset" from the latest issue of *Black Ace* magazine; it was set in Los Angeles, California, and involved the dastardly plans of an evil Oriental criminal mastermind and his cohort of brainwashed underlings. The sharp *rat-a-tat* knock brought Trey back, somewhat unwillingly, to reality.

T. Drummond MacIntyre II popped his head round the door. "Are you ready to go?"

"Me?" Trey jumped up, story forgotten. "Go where? I thought Gramps was coming here."

"Change of plan, we're going there now."

"But I'm..."

"Your grandfather persuaded me that I should allow you this treat, especially as your latest report card showed a distinct improvement on its predecessor."

294

"Hot dog!"

"Just a second..." Trey's father came into the room and surveyed his son and heir. "Run a comb through your hair, straighten your tie and don't forget your jacket; the car's being brought round to the front, so let's get a move on. And, in case you were wondering, I'm driving."

Wetting his comb under the tap and hauling it through his hair, Trey wondered if his pop was *ever* going to let him forget what he'd gotten up to in *Escape from Fox Lake* (as he'd decided to call the story of what happened just a week ago, when he got round to writing it).

Trey's grandparents had a very nice row house on West Eugenie Street, less than fifteen minutes away. But, there having been an auto accident on one of the main cross streets, it was nearly twenty-five minutes later that Trey and his parents were walking up the steps to the ornate front door.

Abigail, the maid, answered the bell and let them in, saying they should go straight down to the back lounge, where Mr. MacIntyre was waiting for them.

"Everyone else is here," Abigail said, closing the front door.

"Who's this 'everyone else', Pop?"

"Wait and see." Trey's father smiled; he knew those

were, used in that particular order, three of his son's least favourite words.

Fully aware that it would be worse than useless to ask any more questions, Trey picked up his pace and strode ahead down the corridor towards the half-open door. Slowing as he got to it, he knocked, as required by family tradition, and went on in; what he saw stopped him dead in his tracks.

"At last!" Gramps stood, a cheroot clamped in his jaw, his thumbs firmly anchored in his waistcoat pockets. He smiled broadly at his grandson. "The guest of honour has arrived!"

"Apologies for the delay, there was a collision on West Oak and LaSalle." Trey's father came and stood next to his stunned offspring. "Are you going to do the introductions, Dad?"

"Of course, of course, I was forgetting that, *you*," Ace MacIntyre pointed at his son, "don't know most of the assembled company! So, may I introduce Robertson Bonner – who, of course, you know by reputation; Captain Maynard, who works with Bob at the Bureau; Mr. Frederick Pisbo, of Pisbo Investigations, Inc., and his daughter Velma, not forgetting Banjo—"

"My mom is still away," Velma butted in, "and he *hates* being left at home by himself."

"Just so, just so, my dear!" Gramps nodded at Banjo.

"Although I'm afraid he'll have to stay here during lunch; the good Mrs. MacIntyre does *not* allow pets in the dining room."

The shock of seeing these people, who'd all played a part in the events of that extraordinary Saturday afternoon up in Fox Lake, had left Trey unusually tongue-tied. Then he noticed an absentee. "Where's Shady?"

"Ah yes, Mr. Jones..." Gramps struck a match and relit his cheroot. "He was invited, but I am informed by Fred – may I call you Fred?" Gramps glanced at Mr. Pisbo, who nodded his assent. "I am informed by Fred that Mr. Jones has – how did he put it, Fred?"

"Well..."

Velma leaped into the gap created by her father's hesitant reply. "He said no offence, *but* he had a reputation to maintain in this burg, something which being seen in the company of officers of the law, and suchlike, would make it hard for him to do."

"Ha-ha!" Gramps threw his head back as he guffawed. "Sounds like a character, our Mr. Jones, shame he couldn't see his way clear to being here with us today."

"But why *are* we all here today, Gramps?" Trey looked round the room, unable to fathom what was up, and why *he* was the "guest of honour". Especially considering he was grounded.

Gramps didn't answer; instead he set about consulting his gold pocket watch. "Shall we all go through to the dining room? I have a feeling luncheon is about to be served."

"But Gramps...!"

"All in good time, son..."

There was something about the way his gramps looked at him that made Trey realize that patience (*not* one of his virtues) was what was called for now.

"Right..." Ace MacIntyre went across to a nearby table, picked up a polished brass bell with an ebony handle and rang it. "Chow time, as they say down on the ranch!"

35 ALL TIED UP

Quite how he managed to contain himself during the meal, Trey did not know. He supposed it could have had something to do with sitting between Mr. Robertson Bonner and his gramps, and opposite his mother, father and Gramma Cecilia. Best behaviour called for, every which way he looked.

He had so many questions that needed answering it was making his hair itch just thinking about it. Compiling a list in his head helped, but not much. And if he said a word he knew the reply would be "All in good time", so he kept his trap shut.

As coffee was being served, to those who wanted it, Gramps stood up, cleared his throat and tapped a glass with the blade of a silver cheese knife. "I think it is about time I put a certain young person of my acquaintance..." he patted Trey on the shoulder, "...out of his most *obvious* misery, and explain to him exactly why we are all here gathered today.

"It is a universal truth that you cannot make an omelette without breaking some eggs, and it is, in my experience, also true that *some* rules are there for the purpose of being broken. The trick, I have found over the years, is to discover which they are – and then not get caught breaking them. Something that, more by luck than judgement I think it fair to say, young Trey here managed to do this summer whilst down at the Circle M."

"I did?" Trey looked up at his grandfather. "Which ones?"

"There was only *one* infringement – that I know of." Gramps raised an eyebrow, to general amusement. "Concerning the T-Bone ranch..."

"Oh, *that* rule..." Trey felt his cheeks colour. "Sorry, Gramps..."

"No need to apologize." Ace MacIntyre patted his grandson's shoulder. "I did have it in for that knucklehead

Bowyer Dunne, but then he *was* trying everything he could to get me to sell him the ranch, cutting fences and such."

"That was him?" Trey queried. "Bowyer Dunne was the barbarian, hooligan saboteur, Gramps?"

"Sure was, son." Ace MacIntyre nodded, tickled pink to hear his own words coming back at him. "He figured it'd be easy to bamboozle an old man, but he hadn't reckoned with me – or you, for that matter, Trey! Truth is, if you hadn't ignored my edicts and gone to that party at the T-Bone, certain situations would be markedly different than they are today – correct, Bob?"

"Indubitably, Ace." Mr. Robertson Bonner leaned back in his chair, nodding in agreement. "Taking those pictures certainly put more than one cat amongst the pigeons – as Mr. Dunne, before he'd sobered up properly, was only too ready to explain!"

"How's that, sir?" Trey frowned. He was having a deal of trouble taking in everything he was being told and wished he hadn't forgotten Austin J. Randall's Number 1 rule: always carry a notebook and pencil!

"Well, son, I can tell by the look on your face that this is all about as clear as a stirred-up muddy pond to you," Mr. Bonner said. "So would you like to hear the story, as far as we all have been able to make it out?"

"You bet!" Trey sat bolt upright, alert as a gundog

who's just heard a 12-bore being loaded.

"Captain Maynard?" Mr. Bonner enquired. "As you've been running this case, would you mind taking over?"

"It'd be my pleasure, sir." Captain Maynard sat back and shot his cuffs. "Right from the start, Trey, it was your sharp eyes that set this whole investigation rolling."

"Really – me?"

"If *you* hadn't told your grandfather about seeing that Buick with the flat tyre – and then that you'd spotted it again at the T-Bone ranch – *he* wouldn't have called my boss and the Bureau wouldn't have begun looking at the connections between Bowyer Dunne and Mario Andrusa." Captain Maynard smiled at Trey. "And, as Mr. Bonner said, the pictures you took at the birthday party sure did get *every*one worked up."

"They did?"

"Seems Mr. Dunne thought your grandfather had sent you to spy on him, and he became convinced Mr. MacIntyre was going to use the pictures of him with a gangster in the papers."

"A *spy*? Me?"

"That's what Dunne told us." Captain Maynard took a moment to light a cigarette. "But there's another twist, because it turns out Mario Andrusa also had his own, very personal reasons for not wanting anyone to see the snaps you took...something to do with the lady he was with not being his wife.

"In fact, Andrusa got *so* worked up when he found out about the snaps, Mr. Dunne panicked, lied through his teeth and told Mario that he'd already gotten hold of the pictures and destroyed them. So he really was desperate to get them back, which is why he dispatched those two fellows that broke into your apartment."

"You mean the cop who got shot *wasn't* a cop?" Trey was stunned at the news; Captain Maynard shook his head. "Gee, all this trouble over a couple of pictures – who'da thought, huh?"

"Who indeed." Captain Maynard tapped some ash off his cigarette, then continued addressing his audience. "It wasn't until we'd finally persuaded Mr. Dunne to turn State's Evidence and spill the beans that we realized Mario Andrusa was still going to want those pictures back. And that he'd most likely think Trey still had them. Trouble was, we didn't get that information until—"

"You mean Andrusa could send someone to get them?" Trey's father interrupted, eyes widened with shock.

"Not could, Mr. MacIntyre. He already did."

"What?!" Trey's mother's complexion paled noticeably.

Captain Maynard coughed and straightened his tie. "You didn't say anything about this yet, Trey?"

Trey's father pinned him with a look. "Speak up, Trey."

"Um, well...you *had* said that the topic of conversation was banned, Pop."

"We – Sophia and I – well, we felt that enough had been said," Trey's father explained, looking at his own father for support. "I didn't think any more talk about the incident would help get things back into a proper perspective. Exactly *what* haven't you told us, Trey?"

"Just that Alex came by the apartment on Monday after school."

"What for?"

"To say goodbye, Pop. You know, as he was going back to New York. Except the *real* reason Alex turned up was to buy the negatives off me. He'd been asked to get them by his Uncle Mario. But as Alex didn't know Mr. Pisbo already had a full set of the photos, I gave them to him, gratis, along with all the other prints I'd made. Seemed like the best thing to do...seeing as if Mr. Andrusa knows for sure *I* don't have them any more, why would he come looking for them again?"

T. Drummond MacIntyre II looked at his son in speechless amazement.

"We came as soon as we found out, Mr. MacIntyre, but that was Tuesday morning; you'd left early, apparently, and Trey here was about to go to school."

Captain Maynard stubbed out his cigarette. "He told us what had occurred, and I have to say, I think he was right on the nail with what he did – Andrusa thinks he's home clean, and we know he isn't. Good work, Trey!"

Gramps stood and grasped Trey's shoulder. "Well I think we should raise a glass in a toast to my grandson – he's a chip off this old block, no doubt about it!" As Gramps raised his glass Trey saw the maid, Abigail, come up and whisper something in his ear. "One final announcement, folks: I've just been informed that a guest who couldn't get here before is waiting in the lounge, so I think we should all go and join him!"

Walking into the lounge Trey saw a man in a brown check suit standing with his back to the room looking out of the window at the garden; he turned as everyone came in, revealing himself to be a florid-faced, slightly portly gentleman with a fine salt-and-pepper walrus mustache that completely hid his mouth.

"Mr. Randall! Pleased to meet you!" Gramps strode across the room, hand outstretched. "So glad you could make it. May I introduce you to my grandson, T. Drummond MacIntyre III?"

"I am delighted to make your acquaintance, young sir, heard a lot about you!" The man grabbed Trey's hand and pumped it for all he was worth. "Austin J. Randall, at your service!"

Trey was still dumbstruck at the idea that right here in front of him was the actual man who had written *How to Become a Private Eye in 10 Easy Lessons* – which, to be honest, was astonishing enough – when Mr. Pisbo appeared, shouting "Jeff! What're *you* doing here?" and things proceeded to get stranger still.

Austin J. Randall gave Mr. Pisbo a massive bear hug and then held him at arm's length, saying how much he hadn't changed. Mr. Pisbo politely begged to differ, but admitted that it was great to meet up again after so long; he patted Austin J. Randall on the back and said what a guy he was, and how much he owed him and that he thought he'd moved to Detroit. Trey was about to pinch himself when someone tapped him on the shoulder.

"My dad used to work for him."

Trey looked round to see Velma and Banjo. "What?"

"Austin J. Randall was his first boss."

"But how..."

"Trey, my boy!" Austin J. Randall grabbed Trey's arm. "Introduce me to your friend, why don't you!"

"I'm Velma Pisbo." Velma stuck her hand out. "And this is my dog Banjo. My dad has mentioned you somewhat more than now and then; pleased to meet you."

"Likewise, my dear, very much likewise!" Austin J.

Randall beamed at Velma and then turned his attention back to Trey. "You look like someone who could do with an explanation, am I right?"

"I should say so – how on earth...?" Trey looked at Mr. Pisbo.

"Nothing to do with me, son. I'm as surprised to see this particular gentleman as you are."

"It's all down to your grandfather, young man." Austin J. Randall tucked both thumbs into his waistcoat pockets. "He told me that he'd noticed you had a copy of my book and that you seemed to be pretty fond of it. That's why he did a bit of detective work of his own; he tracked me down, got in touch and here I am. Hope I'm not a disappointment in the flesh!"

"No sir!"

"That's swell!" Gramps's eyes twinkled, delighted his plan had worked. "Thought the chance to meet your favourite author would be right up your alley!"

"Got something for you, young man – a signed first edition of my book that you might like for your bookshelves. I'll go and get it!"

"Signed! Thanks a lot, sir, that's great." As Trey watched Austin J. Randall hurry off, Mr. Robertson Bonner came up next to him.

"Got my own small token of appreciation for you, son." He reached into his jacket pocket as he spoke and brought out a leather-covered box. "I do believe you more than deserve this."

"What is it, sir?"

"Take a look."

Trey opened the hinged lid to find a brass shield, topped by an American eagle, resting on dark blue silk; he couldn't believe his eyes.

"It's a special presentation Bureau of Investigation badge, son. It ain't real, but I do believe *you* have the makings of a real detective." Mr. Bonner shook Trey by the hand. "I look forward to you joining us!"

Trey stared at the badge. In his head he heard himself announcing "Captain MacIntyre, Bureau of Investigation!" to a bunch of crooks he'd just caught in the act, and he had to admit the words had a real ring to them!

GRAHAM MARKS had his first book of poetry published while he was at art school, studying graphic design. After a successful career as an art director he decided it was time for a change and now works as a journalist and author. He has written everything from comic strips and film tie-ins to advertising copy and novels for children and young adults.

Graham is married to fellow journalist and author Nadia Marks, and lives in London with his two sons and a cat called Boots.

Find out more about Graham Marks at
www.marksworks.co.uk

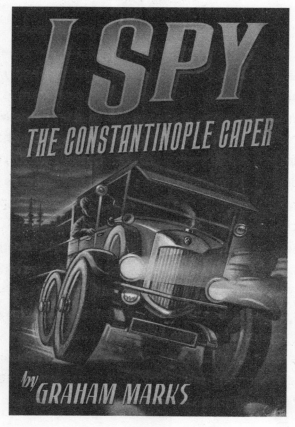

I SPY

Trey can't wait to go on a grand tour of Europe with his father – until he realizes it involves dusty museums and boring business meetings. Then, out of the blue, everything changes and they're boarding the Orient Express, destination: Constantinople. And he's sure they're being followed by a sinister man with a pencil mustache... Who is this shadowy stranger?

Trey feels like his personal hero – star sleuth Trent "Pistol" Gripp, from *Black Ace* magazine – with his own mystery to solve!

But it's a mystery that's about to turn deadly – when Trey finds himself on his own, and on the run, in a city that he soon discovers has a thousand hidden dangers...

"An absolutely gripping spy adventure packed full of mystery, intrigue and high-paced drama."
Lovereading4kids.co.uk

ALSO BY GRAHAM MARKS

ISBN: 9780746068403

**Shortlisted for the North East Children's Book
Award, the Cumbrian Schools' Book Award
and the Rotherham Children's Book Award**

SNATCHED!

Daniel never knew his real parents – abandoned in a lion's cage as a baby, he was adopted into Hubble's travelling circus. When he suffers terrible visions of the future he desperately tries to change what he sees. But he cannot avoid being snatched away to London, where it seems he may have the chance to unlock the riddle of his past. Will he like the answers he finds?

Action-packed, filled with drama and excitement, *Snatched!* takes you on a helter-skelter journey – from the breathtaking theatrics of the circus ring to the very real perils lurking on the streets of Victorian London.

"Graham Marks' racy prose barely lets the reader draw breath. Snatched! is as taut as a highwire and as much fun as a buggy full of clowns."
Meg Rosoff

ALSO BY GRAHAM MARKS

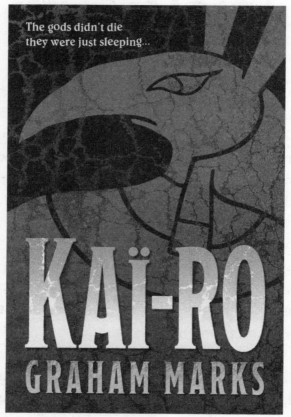

Longlisted for the UKLA Literary Award

KAÏ-RO

Stretch Wilson's world is a hard place. All he has, since his father was taken as slave labour, is his dog, Bone – until the fateful day when he discovers something extraordinary deep in the heart of Bloom's Mount, a gigantic pile of ancient rubbish and waste. Something that will change his life for ever.

Battle is inevitable as the sun rises on a world where once again Setekh, God of Chaos, and Horus, God of the Sky, walk the land. And now Stretch is the only person who can stop the evil that lives in Kaï-ro from taking control, for eternity.

"With a touch of post-apocalypse adventure, a sprinkling of ancient gods, the addition of a likeable boy and his dog, and some storytelling magic, Graham Marks mixes up a novel to be devoured in one sitting."
Garth Nix

FOR MORE UNMISSABLE ACTION
AND ADVENTURE, READ...

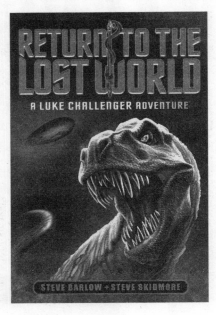

ISBN: 9781409520177

When Luke Challenger's mother is kidnapped, Luke is determined to rescue her – even if it means evading assassins and fighting his way through the deepest Brazilian jungle to brave the Lost World...where real dinosaurs still roam.

Don't miss Luke Challenger's next adventure
RETURN TO
20,000 LEAGUES UNDER THE SEA

ISBN: 9781409508571

A meteorite has struck earth, unleashing an alien virus with strange side effects: superpowers. Sarah and Robert are just two of the kids who must learn to control their new-found powers if they are to escape the clutches of HIDRA, a rogue international agency determined to exploit them...

And Sarah and Robert return to defend the earth in

ALIEN STORM

FOR MORE THRILLING ADVENTURES,
CHECK OUT
WWW.FICTION.USBORNE.COM